CHASING the KING of HEARTS

HANNA KRALL

Translated from the Polish by Philip Boehm
Afterword by Mariusz Szczygieł

FEMINIST
PRESS
AT THE CITY UNIVERSITY
OF NEW YORK
NEW YORK CITY

Published in 2017 by the Feminist Press
at the City University of New York
The Graduate Center
365 Fifth Avenue, Suite 5406
New York, NY 10016

feministpress.org

First Feminist Press edition 2017

 This book was made possible thanks to a grant from New
York State Council on the Arts with the support of Governor
Andrew Cuomo and the New York State Legislature.

 This book is supported in part by an award from the National
Endowment for the Arts.

First printing February 2017

Cover and text design by Suki Boynton

Library of Congress Cataloging-in-Publication Data is available for this title.

CHASING the KING of HEARTS

Shoelaces

She buys shoelaces for a pair of men's shoes—such a trivial purchase.

As she's buying them, she still thinks she's in love with Jurek Szwarcwald. Everybody thinks that, especially Jurek's parents. Jurek isn't ugly and he isn't boring. He isn't poor, either. Izolda is wearing his shoes because a bomb destroyed the house on Ogrodowa Street and now she can't get into her apartment, let alone her wardrobe.

She stops at her friend Basia Maliniak's. Just for a moment, to thread the new laces.

A young man is standing by the stove, warming his hands on the tiles. He's tall and slender, with straight, golden hair. His hands have a golden tinge. When he sits down he spreads his legs and drops his arms—nonchalantly, almost absentmindedly. His hands just hang there, helpless, and even more beautiful. She learns he has two first names, Yeshayahu Wolf, and that Basia calls him Shayek.

She takes her time lacing her shoes. After an hour Shayek says: You have the eyes of a rabbi's daughter. An hour later he adds: A skeptical rabbi.

Basia sees her to the door and hisses: I could kill you right now.

Engaged

He drops by a few days later, with bad news about Hala Borensztajn's brother Adek. (Izolda shared a desk with Hala all through high school.) Adek's dead. From typhus. She can't believe it: typhus? People die of scarlet fever or pneumonia but not from typhus. Shayek says: Now they'll be dying differently, we better get used to that.

They walk over to Hala's. Adek's friends have come as well. The apartment is cold. They drink tea. Basia Malin-iak is knitting a colorful sweater from unraveled yarn and doesn't say a word to either of them. The others talk about typhus. Supposedly it comes from lice. Not from people? No, just lice. Hala laughs at her father, who wants to build a shelter and hide from the lice and from the war. His daughter assures him that the war won't last long, but he's already stocking up on provisions.

The talk moves to love. Izolda says: You know what? I thought I was in love with Jurek Szwarcwald but I was wrong. Should I tell him or not? After some debate her friends conclude that would be too cruel. Get engaged to someone else, they advise, and Shayek tosses out: I'm available. After he leaves, Basia Maliniak puts down her knitting and says: He meant that—and she's right.

The Zachęta Guest House

They take a local train. She opens the window and warm, spring-like air flows inside. The train passes Józefów. She points out the road the old peasant wagon used to take coming from town. You can see how it follows the tracks. Always around this time of year. That's where it turned behind the trees. You can't see the houses from the train. The one with the big porch belongs to the Szwarcwalds. The wagon would drive up and the servant girl would unload all the baskets packed with linens, summer clothes, pots, buckets, brushes. Then she'd fetch water from the well and scrub the floors. At the end of summer the same wagon would drive back in from town and the servant girl would load up all the baskets packed with linens, pots, brushes. There used to be a sandy glade in the woods, not far off, with an old oak tree. No, of course you can't see the tree. It always had so many acorns.

She talks and talks, hoping the words will drown out her fear, as well as her embarrassment and curiosity. They get off at Otwock, the end of the line. A group of older boys scramble out of the next carriage, all very serious and conspiratorial, probably scouts. Their leader issues a few quiet commands—fall in, compasses, northeast—and the column fades into the woods. A freckle-faced boy with a broad smile brings up the rear.

The Zachęta guest house smells of warm pine. Inside the room, Shayek clearly knows what to do with a woman who's as eager as she is afraid, as curious as she is embarrassed. Later that afternoon they head back, stopping to rest under a tree. She lays her head on his lap. They hear a chorus of voices, not very loud, singing a scouting song: *Hur-rah hur-rah, hoo-ray hoo-ray! As long as we can, let's seize the day!*—the boys from the next carriage are also returning to the station. The freckle-faced boy again brings up the rear, but he isn't singing; maybe he doesn't have the voice for it. The boy notices them. Hey, he shouts, take a look at this, the Yids are making love. The boy snickers, then turns around and catches up with his colleagues. Izolda keeps her eyes closed and whispers: Your hair is so blond and your skin is so light, but they could tell. He drapes her sweater around her shoulders. She hadn't realized it had slipped, exposing the armband with the blue star.

A Sign

They get married. She wears a sky-blue dress tinged with lilac. Her mother bought the fabric a long time ago, thinking she would sew something to wear for her son's birthday dinner. The color was pervenche—very much in vogue because Wallis Simpson was so fond of it. The duchess had worn periwinkle when she married Edward VIII, or maybe it was to the banquet afterward. In the end Mother didn't sew anything because her two-year-old son died of pneumonia. She dressed in black and announced she would wear mourning for the rest of her life.

Thanks to Jurek Szwarcwald (he was surprisingly quick to accept her breaking it off and he too got married; his wife, Pola, was a nice, smart woman and by no means unattractive despite a longish nose)—thanks to Jurek, who's studying medicine, Izolda lands a job in a hospital, looking after the typhus patients. She gives them water with valerian, massages their bedsores, and straightens their pillows. For the first time in her life she sees corpses (which are carried off to the cemetery in wooden handcarts with two large wheels on both sides and four handles for pulling). She has yet to witness someone dying and she very much wants to. She's not so curious about what visions the dying person might have—light, dark, angel, or God—but wants to know what she might see when someone else's life comes to an end. A soul? A sign? Because if there is a sign, it ought to be read. She sits beside a young girl, very beautiful despite her illness. She keeps watch all night long, and just as the day breaks she hears a quiet sighing. The sick girl's chest rises—and doesn't fall. Izolda leans over the girl, alert and concentrated. She examines the girl's face—peaceful, serious—but sees no sign of a soul. They load the girl's body onto the black wooden wagon. Izolda takes off her apron and goes home. She tells her husband what death looks like: no soul, no sign. Then she adds, by way of encouragement: We're still alive, though. To which her husband says: Even that is less and less certain.

The Source of Optimism

At night she works in private homes. These patients are well-off, they have their own clean sheets, their own doctor, and a genuine funeral. They also have a separate grave. Whoever can't afford a grave or a funeral is taken out to the street, where the body must be covered with sheets of newspaper. The paper has to be weighed down against the wind with a brick or a stone.

There's a lot to be learned from these newspaper shrouds.

Who counts as a Jew (anyone with three Jewish grand-parents).

Where to wear the armband with the star (on the right sleeve only).

What kind of armbands are to be worn by ragmen and waste collectors (red violet—the green ones used up until now are no longer valid).

What the March ration cards are good for (five hundred grams of sauerkraut and one hundred grams of beetroot), what the April cards are worth (one box of forty-eight matches), and what can be expected in December (one egg with an oval stamp on the shell).

How to make soup out of leftover bread (soak in water, boil, strain, and add saccharin).

What kind of saccharin is kosher for Passover (as decreed by the rabbinate, only in crystal form, dissolved and run through a sieve before the holiday).

Where Dr. Korczak will be telling children stories (the orphanage on Śliska Street).

What kind of crime Moszek Goldfeder committed (he passed a woman on the street, grabbed her loaf of bread, and took off, eating as he ran; when brought before the Jewish police he apologized to the victim and promised to change for the better).

Where to mend clothes (nowhere but the Keller workshop, because they hire pedantic old spinsters).

Where to arrange for a hearse (nowhere but Eternity, the company that invented the bicycle-cart hearse—very practical, it can carry up to four coffins at once!).

The source of Jewish optimism (it comes from being created in God's image—the fount of all goodness and the source of all being, without beginning).

No one in her family has died yet. Her father traded half an apartment building for a whole calf's hide. Her mother trades pieces of the hide for onions and bread.

The Padlock

She needs to borrow a little money. She goes to Hala Borensztajn (the one she sat next to all through high school). Fifty? What do you need fifty zlotys for? Hala's father is surprised. Izolda explains that it's for the German guard: he looks the other way and I walk out of the ghetto. That costs fifty whole zlotys. You want to leave? Hala is astounded. With your hair? Hala herself is blond and has a snub nose, but she has no intention of leaving their shelter before the war is over. She shows off the tap with water, the bags of grain, and the stock of medicine. Izolda agrees, the shelter is fantastic, so, now will you lend me the money? Mr. Borensztajn hands her ten zlotys and she promises to return them when the war is over. She borrows forty from Halinka Rygier's father (Halinka sat right behind Hala in school) and then hurries to her husband.

Her husband works in a factory set up in the attic of a multistory apartment building. She hears the rumble of trucks as she climbs the stairs. At the top of the stairs a man is putting a padlock on the door to the workshop. His hand is shaking and he has trouble fitting the key into the lock. Where's Shayek? she asks the man. In there—he points at the door (the hand he uses to point is also shaking) and then runs downstairs. Shayek, she whispers to the lock, I can't get in. The motors get louder and louder. Shayek! She tries to break the padlock, punches it with all her strength. Shayek, I can't just stand here! In the court-yard someone shouts, "Jews come out!" and she hears the stamping of feet. She knows what's coming next: they'll search the apartments, floor by floor. They're going to find me, she explains to the lock. They're going to find me and take me to Umschlagplatz. She hears a child crying, then several shots and a quavering voice she doesn't recognize: Save me! Shayek, save me! When she hears "Shayek" she realizes that the voice is her own. That's me crying out, I just got a little scared, but now I'm calm, I can't stay here because they'll shoot me, I can't stay here, they'll shoot me on the spot, he'll open the door and then what, he'll see me shot dead, I can't . . . She says all that out loud as she runs down the stairs. In front of the building Jewish policemen and SS men are lining everyone up in a column. One of the policemen is Jurek Gajer, who recently married Basia Maliniak. He notices Izolda and lifts his hands to say: I can't do anything to help you, you see for yourself, and places her in the column. They march off down the empty streets and through a wide-open wooden gate. They pass the hospital and stop at the collection point. She thinks: This is Umschlagplatz and this is where I am. The cattle wagons will come for us . . . My God, they'll come to take us away—and how will he manage without me?

Left Hemisphere

The film is playing in slow motion and the sound has been turned down—that's why everyone is moving more slowly and speaking more quietly. Or not speaking at all, they're just sitting on their bags and rocking back and forth, back and forth. Or they're whispering to themselves, very possibly praying. They've calmed down, stopped bustling about—there's no more running away. They wait. They don't have the strength for anything else.

She is unable to wait. (By now the roundup must be over, the man has unlocked the door, and the workers have come out of the factory. Are you Shayek? the man asks. Your wife was here . . . Shayek runs down onto the street, Iza, he calls out, Izolda, and Jurek Gajer repeats: Izolda's gone, she went to Umschlagplatz . . . Stop shouting, listen to me, Izolda isn't here.)

Izolda looks around. There's a barrel next to the wall. She can tell at a glance that it's too small, but she tries to climb inside anyway. The barrel flips over and so does she. The hospital is locked, but even so she stands near the entrance and waits there for hours. A doctor from the typhus ward looks out of the window and sees her. That's our nurse, he tells the policeman. They let her in, she lies down on an empty bed. Surely they won't take the sick people, she thinks, but someone enters the room and announces that they're taking all the patients. She gets up and mops the floor, thinking they won't take away the orderlies, but someone enters the room . . . She puts on a white apron, they won't take the nurses . . . A Jewish policeman lines up all the workers and holds out his cap. People toss in rings, necklaces, watches . . . Izolda takes out the silver compact Shayek had given her as an engagement present. She opens it, wipes the powder off the mirror, checks herself, and tosses it into the cap. The policeman picks up the compact and returns it without a word, he's not interested in silver. They're allowed to leave the hospital. Umschlagplatz is now empty. A few people are scurrying through the streets. The wind picks up newspapers, bangs on abandoned pots, slams open windows. A horse whinnies somewhere close by. Lying on the pavement is an overturned bowl, white pockmarked with black where the enamel chipped off—a bowl someone had wanted to take along but it was too unwieldy for the journey.

Izolda tells her parents she isn't spending another day in the ghetto. That's right, you're absolutely right, her father agrees, making a slight gesture with the thumb and forefinger of his right hand. She knows that gesture, that's how her father underscores his pronouncements. You're not going to your death like some docile little lamb, he states in a solemn voice, raising his right hand once again. She's not thinking about how she will go to her death. She isn't going to her death. She's thinking about her father's reflexive gesture, how it originates in the left hemisphere of the brain, which is responsible for speech and the movements of the right limbs. She learned about reflexes at nursing school, but can people on the Aryan side distinguish between the workings of the left hemisphere and Jewish gesticulation? It's good you're getting out of here, he assures her, and hugs her tightly, so that his hands are behind her back. And because his hands are behind her back, she doesn't have to wonder what people might think who don't know about the workings of cerebral hemispheres.

Early the next morning her husband accompanies her to the guard post.

She takes out the money she borrowed from Mr. Rygier and Mr. Borensztajn, hands fifty zlotys over to the guard, and walks out of the ghetto with a calm, unhurried step.

Armchair. Rose Marie

At some point—about a quarter of a century after the war—she will begin to imagine her old age.

She will sit in her armchair (lemon, olive, and almond trees will be growing outside her window).

She will reach for a book, one of many that she promised herself she would read someday.

She will watch a film, one of many that . . .

She'll put on a record . . .

She will go for a long walk up Mount Carmel. Perhaps

she'll head down to the beach, take off her slippers, feel the moist sand under her feet, warmer than the sand in Sopot, but a little coarser . . .

In the evening one of her granddaughters will stop by and talk about work. About school. About her boyfriend. I thought I was in love with him, she'll confess to her grandmother in secret, but I was wrong.

Izolda will try to tell her granddaughter an extraordinary story from half a century earlier (what else?) and her granddaughter will sit at her knees and listen eagerly. Finally she'll shut her eyes and whisper: And that was that. Just like in the American film *Rose Marie* from before the war, based on Friml's operetta, starring Jeanette MacDonald and Nelson Eddy. Rose Marie, old but still beautiful, sits in her armchair and tells her story, while the film replays her entire life. Except that MacDonald didn't close her eyes. That was Vivien Leigh as Lady Hamilton, in a completely different film, but no matter. In the last paragraph of the book that someone will write about her life, she could repeat: And that was that—her eyes closed in meditation.

Armchair. The Foreign-Language Teacher

In what language will she tell these stories? Her grandchildren won't understand Polish, and she won't ever master Hebrew, so maybe English? After all, she took lessons at the Szwarcwalds' three times a week for three months from a private tutor hired by Jurek's mother . . . The man had a brilliant method: at their very first lesson he read Oscar Wilde out loud to his students, in English: *High above the city, on a tall column, stood the statue of the Happy Prince* . . . the beginning of his favorite story, "The Happy Prince." He was an elderly bachelor, somewhat shy and very polite. When he sat down to eat he bowed to everyone and said, "Bon appétit," and after they'd finished he bowed again and said, "Thank you very much." Mrs. Szwarcwald served him dinner in exchange for the lesson. Izolda learned fast and worked hard (she lined her notebook very neatly, filling the columns with irregular verb forms: *to be—was—been; to eat—ate—eaten*) and would have certainly mastered English if the teacher hadn't hanged himself. The paper mentioned a middle-aged man committing suicide, but the notice didn't give a last name, so she couldn't be sure it was him. The column "Unhappy Accidents" frequently listed similar incidents, while the "First Aid" column offered medical advice, which in the case of hangings was to administer artificial respiration immediately after cutting the person down. Unfortunately, the brilliant teacher wasn't cut down in time and artificial respiration was not administered, so Izolda R. will be able to say *High above the city, on a tall column* . . . but won't be able to tell the story of her life to her granddaughter sitting at her knees.

The Handbag

. . . she hands fifty zlotys to the guard and walks out of the ghetto with an unhurried step.

She carries a handbag (which her mother bought for her at Herse's right before graduation) and a small beach bag containing a nightdress, a toothbrush, and her favorite yellow beach robe, which can also double for indoor use.

She knocks, the door opens, and standing at the threshold is Captain Szubert's wife, Kazimiera, their neighbor from the summer house at Józefów, whom everyone calls Lilusia. Lilusia is already dressed. She's tied her braid up in a bun and is holding a cigarette. She's neither surprised nor frightened. Come in, she says, and quickly chains the door. And don't cry, please, we mustn't cry. "We," she says. To a person who shouts "save me" to a padlock. Who tries to hide in an undersized barrel. The wife of a Polish officer (her husband is a prisoner of war in Germany, she has a weapon hidden inside the folding table and underground newspapers in the sofa bed) and she says, "We."

Izolda stops crying and eats breakfast. She feels increasingly better. Part of a better world—an Aryan world, tasteful and tidy.

A hairdresser friend treats her hair. First he bleaches out her natural color with peroxide and then he dyes it ash blond. She looks in the mirror, pleased: that's perfect, not like all those other little Jewish girls with hair as yellow as straw.

She has nothing in common with the straw color of those other little Jewish girls. She becomes a blond, and a tall one at that, because her long, sturdy legs give her height. Satisfied, she returns to Lilusia Szubert.

Lilusia has company: the caretaker of the building and his son. It's secret school in the kitchen, today's subject is Polish history: King Władysław Jagiełło fought, conquered, and died . . . Where did he die? asks Lilusia. Władysław Jagiełło died in Gródek, very good, on the Wereszyca River, tomorrow we'll look it up on the map, and what happened next? The boy doesn't know what happened next, so Izolda excuses the interruption, greets the guests, and drops her bag on the table, the carefree gesture of a tall blond. Lilusia breaks off the lesson: Maria, take that handbag off the table, you can't go tossing your bag around like some Jew girl. Izolda quickly picks up her handbag, excuses herself, and laughs out loud with all the others. The guests take their leave, and Lilusia explains that she was being crafty, that her remark was meant to clear any suspicions on the part of the caretaker. Izolda understands Lilusia's cunning, but then she takes a closer look at the handbag and sets it on the floor. How's that? Does the bag look Jewish there? She tries the sofa, the stool, the chair. Because if it does, what exactly about the bag is Jewish? The patent leather is thin and soft, the color of café au lait. The finish is scratched up and is coming off in places, but she can't spot anything suspicious about the leather itself. How about the handle? Slightly bent, wrapped with braided silk, a little dirty, but it's probably not about the braid. Or the lining, also silk, which can't even be seen and which her manicure kit has torn in a couple places. Once again: on the floor, the stool, the chair . . . Does the bag look Jewish?

The Voice

Passes for the ghetto are issued at Krasiński Square, inside the old theater warehouse (formerly used for storing sets and costumes). She steps up to the German clerk and introduces herself as Maria Pawlicka. She used to keep house for a Jewish family, she left some of her belongings with them and now she needs them back because she doesn't have a thing. To prove her point she lifts her blouse a bit to show there's nothing underneath. The German looks up from under his glasses. A civilian, completely gray headed except for two tufts of red hair sticking out of his ears. Those hairs make her feel a little safer; they remind her of a doctor she once knew who'd moved from Vilna to be with his grandchildren in Józefów. The doctor used to examine her when she was little, whenever she had bronchitis. He never had his stethoscope with him, so he'd hold his ear against her chest and say breathe,

breathe, in his funny eastern Polish accent. The red hairs sticking out of his ears tickled so much that her mother had to quiet her down.

The German with the same coloring as the doctor from Vilna lowers his glasses and writes out, very meticulously: Maria Pawlicka. She takes her pass and crosses into the ghetto (through the theater warehouse) but right away is stopped by a German gendarme who doesn't like the look of her permit. He rips it in half and sends her back to the Aryan side. She shows the torn pieces to the clerk. So is that all your piece of paper is worth?

She's amazed at her own voice—fast, shrill, all the words in one breath—and is somewhat surprised to recognize the voice of Wandzia, the redheaded daughter of the caretaker at Ogrodowa Street. Izolda had been there once when Wandzia came back from a wedding and immediately wanted something to eat. Didn't they have any food at the wedding? her mother asked. They did, but they didn't exactly force it down our throats, the dogs—and then the girl burst into laughter. Izolda would occasionally imitate that laugh and that voice—high, provocative, self-assured. Just right for a tall blond, she thinks now, with satisfaction, as she places the damaged permit on the German's desk. Repeating his earlier gesture, the clerk lifts his glasses. Without a word he glues the paper back together and stamps it once again. This time they let her in.

She hands the document to her mother and they both

walk out of the ghetto. Her mother by way of the guard post, Izolda through the theater warehouse. The old clerk doesn't stop her, he knows her papers are in order.

The Sisters

They take the train. Izolda's hair is stylishly rolled up at the back. Her mother is dressed in black and is her usual sad, silent self. (Her silence is the good kind, from the old days when—mostly over dessert—she would prop her head on her hands and listen to her husband's tirades on politics or life or love or smiles, especially female smiles—his favorite subject. That and roulette, which he played in Sopot. How the wheel spins and how women smile. The smiles come in two types: consenting and encouraging. And when I see a consenting smile it's impossible for me to back away—he boasted to his wife and daughter and to the young governess. Mother didn't show either type of smile, only a sad grimace, her mouth turned down at the corners.)

Izolda looks cautiously around. Do the passengers realize that her mother's sadness and her black dress come from normal times? That the furrows around her mouth aren't the despair of the ghetto, but simply the bitterness of a wife betrayed? That she's in mourning because of her son, who did not die of starvation or in the cattle car, but simply of pneumonia? In a word, do the passengers crowded into the third-class compartment realize that her mother's black dress and sadness are good, non-Jewish sadness and safe, non-Jewish black?

They arrive at the house of Shayek's two sisters and his little nephew Szymuś. Izolda leaves her mother with them, but that turns out to be a bad idea. The sisters are terrified. A *szmalcownik* spotted them at the station and blackmailed them out of a ring, and they worry he might have followed them home. I'll come back for you as soon as I find another place, she promises her mother. The sisters ask Izolda to look after their brother. And our parents, Hela insists. And our brother, and our youngest sister, Halina. And our parents. Why me? she asks herself in the train on the way back. Absentmindedly she adjusts her hair, which is dyed, in contrast to Hela's, which is real, genuine blond. Why what? asks the conductor. She realizes that she's been talking out loud. She smiles at the conductor: Why nothing, nothing at all.

Bolek

Jurek Szwarcwald has a talent for finding decent people. Not only does he know a doctor who operates on Jews (the man lengthened Jurek's foreskin and shortened Jurek's wife's nose right before he was killed in a public execution in the middle of town), but he also manages to meet Bolek. Bolek crosses into the ghetto several times a week. By day completely legally, with a construction firm sent in to tear down buildings destroyed in the fighting. At night illegally, on other business, through the sewer system.

Jurek tells Izolda where to go and how many times to knock. She finds Bolek in a basement carpentry workshop, full of shavings and sawdust, planes, files. A few men are sitting on a stack of boards, thin, wiry, unshaven, with unbuttoned shirts and not exactly sober.

She explains who sent her.

So? asks Bolek.

She explains that her husband is in the ghetto.

So?

So we have to get him out. We can't use the guard anymore, but my husband could go with you, through the sewers.

With me, love? Bolek gives her a patronizing smile. First someone would have to go and find him, and we can't leave our site. It's dangerous inside the ghetto, love. Terrible things happening there. Who's going to fetch your husband?

I will, she says. I'll go along and bring him to you.

Bolek stops smiling, stops calling her "love." He buttons his shirt and gets up off the boards.

You mean you'll go through the sewers, ma'am?

Where do I meet you? she asks.

A Request

She waits by the manhole. The sun goes down, but there's
no sign of Bolek. Sirens signal an air raid. She heads to
the nearby garrison chapel. She opens the door and takes
a few steps in the dark. A priest is standing in the aisle
holding a book. Just saying my prayers . . . He smiles at
her. They're close to the ghetto wall and can hear single
shots from the other side. My God, the things going on
over there, the priest whispers, and turns his head toward
the shooting. My husband is over there, she whispers. The
priest places his hand on her shoulder and says: I'll pray
for him, what more can I do? And with his other hand,
the one holding the prayer book, he makes a helpless gesture (which reminds her a little of Jurek Gajer before she
was marched off to Umschlagplatz: "I can't do anything
to help you, you see for yourself."). You could give him
a baptismal certificate, Father, she suggests. Just one, for
a young man. The priest doesn't reply. And a place to
stay? The priest thinks for a moment. Please come back,
he says, and breaks out in a violent, hacking cough. Best
would be two places, she quickly adds, speaking over the
cough, but the priest clears his throat, covers his mouth
with a handkerchief, and retreats to the sacristy.

She returns a few days later. She wants to explain to
the priest why she asked for two places to stay. One is for
people with "bad" looks who can't show themselves on

the street, who speak with a strong Yiddish accent; the other is for people with fairly "good" looks who speak proper Polish. The second one, she plans to explain, wouldn't be all that risky.

She asks a nun about the priest: slender, not young, with a persistent cough.

You must mean Father Franciszek, the nun concludes. Franciszek Pauliński. He's in the tuberculosis ward on Wolska Street.

She buys a lemon at the Kiercelak market and goes to the hospital.

The priest is dozing.

She looks at him. He's not going to find any place at all, she thinks sadly. Not for people with "good" looks and not for people with "bad" ones.

It's you . . . The priest opens his eyes and peers at her. Will you pray for me?

For you, Father? Me!

You, child. You won't forget, will you?

She leans over the man's bed.

I'm not a child of the same God as you, Father. That's not a God I turn to. And that God doesn't treat me justly. Or my parents. Or my husband . . .

She speaks louder and louder, with her new, high-pitched, quarrelsome voice. The nurse tells her to be quiet. By the time she leaves she has calmed down: Father Franciszek asked her to pray for him. If the rector of the

Pallottines himself is asking her for such a favor, then it means there's something on this earth that does depend on her. At least a prayer.

She visits him a few times. She brings him a book from the Szuberts' library called *The New Temple*, in which some Norwegian suggests that we seek God in nature, that richest of all tomes. The advice sounds good to Izolda. Sitting on the hospital bed, she reads out loud to the priest: about green meadows embroidered with yellow and pink flowers, about the waves of hills, about azure fjords and verdant fields and migratory birds and the secret resonance of the soul in nature. Unfortunately the priest isn't concerned with birds or fields or fjords. The priest is dying.

Tailors

Every day she stands by the manhole; at last Bolek's people show up. When it gets dark they lift the cover and quickly slip inside. The men have a long rope, which gets looped around each person's waist. The runoff comes up to their calves. They stink. They walk doubled over, carrying full sacks. Izolda touches the rope stretching in front of her and peers into the darkness ahead for signs of a lantern. It doesn't take long. They crawl out onto the street, they're inside the ghetto. They wait in the ruins, and in the morning the Jews appear—silent, unshaven, dirty. They bring overcoats, sheets, tablecloths, porcelain, silverware. Bolek's people take onions, garlic, bread, and bottles of oil out of their sacks and give them to the Jews. To some they give Polish ID cards. What about a place to stay? asks a man with a beard. Do you have an address for me? At least for a few days . . . One of Bolek's workers is surprised: The way you look, are you crazy?—and the Jew nods his head in understanding. When the sacks are empty Bolek's men refill them with Jewish belongings and hide them in the ruins. Then they start to work tearing down what's left of the buildings.

Not far from Izolda's old apartment is a workshop where tailors are sewing German uniforms. She asks about her husband. The tailors saw him on Miła Street, just a few days ago. She asks about her neighbors. Did anyone see the Rygiers? They're gone . . . The tailor who knows about the Rygiers doesn't look up from his sewing machine. Nobody's here, they went to the trains. Szwarcwald? Father or son? Father. Not here. His wife took poison and he went to the trains. He managed to give his keys to some acquaintance. Keys to what? The tailors don't know, maybe to some hidden shelter? Maybe he locked someone inside? Borensztajn? Did you see the Borensztajns? They had a daughter . . . They had a shelter . . . The tailors are calm and matter-of-fact. They're not here, they say. So what if they had a shelter . . . A really good one? So what of it? Not here, understand? The tailors stay hunched over their machines. Now she understands. The others aren't there, but the tailors are. Maybe they will stay. Maybe there won't be any more trains. Maybe, God willing, they'll stay forever?

Father

She makes her way to Miła Street, her anxiety growing with every step. She walks faster and faster and finally breaks out into a run. The other pedestrians also start running. Not because they want to see her husband, they just think they have to. She dashes into an entrance, the others follow. She stops and they stop. I'm running to my husband, she explains. They look at her, bewildered, and disperse.

Her husband is so sleepy he's barely conscious. She strokes his hair, which is no longer golden. Is everybody still here? She wants to make sure. He shakes his head. Your father's gone. He left . . . of his own free will, when they called for specialists.

She begins to understand: her father left the ghetto voluntarily.

I tried to stop him, her husband says, but he said that he'd explain it all to them.

Explain what?

That as a chemist who knew German and a graduate of Heidelberg . . .

But explain what?

That as a chemist . . . I begged him, her husband repeats.

(Her father had pretty, brown, wise eyes.)

They took them to Umschlagplatz, her husband says. Apparently the specialists who knew German were the first to board the train . . .

(One eye was brown; he had lost the other while searching for a new color.

A color that doesn't exist in the spectrum, at least not yet, a color with a new wavelength. He explained that the colors of the spectrum differ from one another by their wavelengths, and that the gamut of wavelengths is matched by the colors given off by all living creatures. Her father loved to explain things, adored explaining things. Colors, smiles, roulette . . . He was on the verge of making a great discovery but an unfortunate explosion ruined everything. So he gave up working on the spectrum and went into business. He started with the tenants who didn't pay their rent and resolved to have a serious conversation with them. You see, he explained to them, above all else a man has to make sure his children have a roof over their heads, that's what makes for a true man. You're absolutely right, Mr. Furman, the tenant agreed, but what if a man doesn't have money for a roof? Then he should borrow it, Father advised. You're absolutely right, the tenant agreed, could you lend me some money so my children can have a roof over their heads? Father lent the money, the tenant paid, Father gave him a receipt, and

Mother suggested that maybe he wasn't cut out for business after all. So Father went to Sopot. From there he sent funny postcards assuring us that he was developing a new method of winning at roulette.)

Izolda doesn't hold it against Shayek that he allowed her father to leave.

Nor is she surprised at how calmly he talks about it. Just like the tailors in the shop: he's gone, too bad, but we're still here.

In the evening they meet up with Bolek.

Before climbing down into the sewer she kneels on a pile of bricks. Ask her . . . she whispers to her husband. Ask who what? Get on your knees and pray . . . She reaches for the Mother of God medallion that Lilusia Szubert gave her (She'll look after you, she said, as she draped the chain around Izolda's neck). Pray that nothing bad happens to us . . . She would like to add: Today and until the end of the war—but she reconsiders, they shouldn't ask for too much. Help us, she says out loud. Please be kind and help us. You won't forget?

Hotel Terminus

Things aren't bad: she rents a room in Wesoła, a town on the outskirts of Warsaw, and fetches her mother. She becomes friends with her neighbor, who has a handicapped child. Mother and daughter spend the day riding the local trains. The daughter sings and the mother collects handouts in a canvas sack. The little girl has a long, thin neck; she leans her small head to the side and sings Brahms's Lullaby with Polish words: *Jutro znów, jak Bóg da, wstaniesz wesół i zdrów* . . . Her voice is high-pitched, perfectly clear, with a nice vibrato.

Izolda returns to the ghetto for some bedding and carries the bundle back out via the theater warehouse. Then she takes a rickshaw to the train station.

A policeman standing at the corner of Świętokrzyska Street and Nowy Świat eyes her closely. He waves the rickshaw to the curb, climbs in, and says something to the driver . . . They turn onto Chmielna Street and stop at the Hotel Terminus. The policeman orders her inside. He takes a key at the reception. Inside the room he looks at her shrewdly and smiles: So what do we have here but a little Jew girl, am I right? Take off your clothes.

She takes off her clothes.

The policeman unbuckles his belt with the holster, takes off his uniform, and shoves her to the bed. His breathing is hoarse, loud, long, he smells of cigarettes and sweat. She thinks: Will he demand money? Take me to the station? Ask for my address? The policeman stops moving. She thinks: Will he follow me to Wesoła? Will he find my mother? The policeman gets up and dresses. He stands in front of the mirror and combs his mustache and hair. Put your clothes on, he says. Now go outside and get back in your rickshaw. You see how lucky you are, running into a decent person . . . He salutes and heads back toward Nowy Świat. The rickshaw driver asks: To the station?

Her neighbor is on the train, with her daughter. The girl is singing, *Jutro znów, jak Bóg da* . . . Izolda tosses five whole zlotys into the canvas sack—she's happy he didn't demand money, didn't take her to the station, didn't ask . . .

She starts to regret that she didn't ask him for anything. At least for a place to stay. Since you are such a decent person, couldn't you find me a safe address . . . Or even two. One for the people who can't show themselves on the street and the other . . . As she washes herself and changes her underwear, she regrets letting such a great opportunity slip by: she ran into a decent person and didn't ask for a thing.

Justice

Shayek leaves to fetch his sisters but comes back without them. They committed suicide, after poisoning little Szymuś. Shayek tried to find out where they were buried, but the man who dug their grave is no longer alive either.

It was Hela, she tells her husband. It had to be Hela. She managed to get her hands on some cyanide. She probably said . . . What would you say in that situation? Let's not . . . Or: This doesn't make sense anymore . . . Maybe

you don't say anything, just reach for the white powder
. . . And Szymuś, Tusia's six-year-old son? Which one of
them said: Be a good boy and swallow it all?

She was so pretty, that Hela. So blond . . . and yet she
didn't want to save herself. And meanwhile she, Izolda,
with dyed hair and eyes a policeman can spot while she's
riding in a rickshaw, she's supposed to save everybody. Is
that fair? she asks her husband. Tell me, where's the justice in that? But her husband asks her not to say anything
against his sisters.

Armchair. Another Stupid Mistake

Her plans for old age turn out to be unrealistic.

She won't read books because she'll lose her eyesight.
She won't listen to records because she'll be hard of

hearing. She won't go on walks because her lower verte-
brae will pinch her lumbar nerves . . .

Her granddaughter, the gallery owner, could come and
tell her about contemporary art.

Her other granddaughter, the cultural historian, could
tell her about the cultures of the world.

Her third granddaughter will be in the army.

But because Izolda doesn't know Hebrew she'll never
learn about contemporary art or what will happen to the
cultures of the world. Her soldier granddaughter will
visit her when she's on leave. She'll take off her boots,
put down her rifle, sit on the sofa, and fall asleep right
away. Izolda will cover up her granddaughter with a plaid
blanket and say in Polish: *Śpij, dziecko*—Sleep, child. And
when she awakes, her granddaughter will get dressed up
and run to meet a boy, who's very handsome even though
he has a large ring under his lip. Izolda would like to
ask if the ring doesn't get in the way of kissing, but once
again she can't remember the Hebrew word for ring. (The
plaid blanket she'll use to cover her granddaughter will be
light and soft but warm, with a colorful pattern, just like
another, very different plaid blanket. She'll try to tell her
granddaughter about that blanket, only she won't be able
to. That one felt safe, peaceful, secure, but what kind of
safety can there be in the Israeli army?)

She'll sit down in her armchair.

She'll start to think. That's all she can do anymore.
And then she'll remember another stupid mistake. For

instance, how could she have put his parents and sisters in with other Jews? The setup was fine, the widow who owned the apartment was an honest woman; the only problem was that her parents had to share it with a young married couple. Both had good papers and decent looks, but the husband was circumcised. Izolda should have found a different flat, with an uncircumcised Jew. Although even an uncircumcised Jew would have been found out (for instance, by running into an acquaintance on the street). She should have avoided places where there were any other Jews at all. Maybe, if she'd asked the policeman from the rickshaw for an apartment without Jews . . . Of course they would have died anyway. (They would have taken shelter in the basement during the Warsaw Uprising and been killed by bombs.) Oh well, she'll console herself, next time I'll be smarter. What am I babbling about, she catches herself, what next time?

The Widow

Her husband's parents spend all day sitting on the floor; they crawl to the bathroom. The honest widow doesn't allow them to walk around the apartment, and she's right: someone in the building opposite could look through the window and see everything. His parents have terrible looks and a terrible accent. They need to be well hidden and the greater the risk, the more you have to pay.

Her husband starts working for Bolek. He's no longer Shayek or Wolf, but Władek. During the day he enters the ghetto and loads bricks onto horse carts; at night he goes back through the sewers to pick up the Jewish belongings stashed in the ruins. He sells them to regular customers, uses the proceeds to buy food for the Jews, and gives what's left to the widow. When the fighting breaks out in the ghetto and he can no longer work day or night, the widow still keeps her lodgers—a magnanimous woman.

Izolda and her husband look at the flames. At the black smoke rising over the wall. They listen to the shooting and guess where the shots are coming from, what is burning, where people are trying to escape. (Will they manage to get out or will they die in the flames?) Every now and then someone walking on the pavement or waiting for the tram turns to them and says: "Holy Jesus, what a terrible thing," or words to that effect, and when that happens they are afraid. Why is the person saying that to them? Dear God, why them? They don't answer, just head off as fast as they can. They want to keep as far as possible from people who are saddened and sympathetic. But if someone says: "Look at those Yids getting fried," then they're calm, because it's clear no one suspects who they are. When that happens they don't hurry away, just stand there: Oh well, they're getting fried all right.

In the middle of May the uprising dies down. Bolek's people return to work. It's high time, the widow is beginning to get impatient.

The Acquaintance

Her husband leads the parents of a friend through the sewers out of the ghetto. They can both pass as Poles. The mother is tall and hefty, the father has a mustache, so it's all right to take them home. (Lilusia found an apartment for Izolda and Shayek on Mariańska Street. The former owners were Jewish and the caretaker, Mateusz, is kind and trustworthy. The place had been looted, but they repaired the windows, put in a stove, and installed a pipe and made themselves at home.)

Everything would be all right if Shayek's friend had sensible parents: the apartment is close to the stairwell and the neighbors can hear every sound. Unfortunately they aren't sensible. They boil water, they bang around lighting the stove, and eventually they have to move out.

Her husband finds them another place and takes them there.

On the street they see an acquaintance, a Jew from Łódź. The acquaintance sees them as well and gives a friendly smile. The couple smile back and go on.

They go inside the apartment. An hour later someone knocks at the door. They look through the peephole: it's the acquaintance from Łódź.

When they open the door they realize he isn't alone but with some policemen, who haul everyone down to the station. There they let Shayek go and take the elderly couple to the Kripo.

The next day her husband wakes up saying that they

have to help those people. Her circumcised husband. Whose papers are forged. Whose wife dyes her hair. Whose parents are hiding under a windowsill. Who has sacks of Jewish belongings stashed in the ruins of the ghetto. And he wants to go to the Kripo. She blocks his way and yells: Why are you going? For whom? You're the one who's supposed to live, not them. He pushes her off and walks out. But he doesn't accomplish anything. Lucky the Germans don't check inside his fly.

A couple of weeks later a card arrives from the camp, with two words: "Save us." Shayek's friend sends a telegram, with six words: "Save them, where to send money?" If they were my parents, Izolda tells her husband, I would get on the train to save them myself, but her husband understands his friend well. She doesn't want to lose her job housekeeping in a German home. She wants to stay there quietly until the end of the war. Shayek is right. His friend will survive, while her parents, who in their desperation were so bold as to put Shayek's life in jeopardy, will die in the camp.

Armchair. A Problem

She should have told her husband to take them one at a time: first the father, then the wife. Or vice versa: first the wife—surely the acquaintance from Łódź wouldn't have recognized her. But he would have spotted the husband, since they had done business together. No, Shayek should have taken the husband first. He would have been caught, but the wife would have survived. Of course she would have been caught too, only later . . . What about the acquaintance from Łódź, did he survive the war? Obviously he was saving himself and those closest to him, every Jewish informer was saving someone. There's just one problem: at what cost do you save yourself? And who thinks about that problem when you have to save someone?

A Virgin

Her husband helps another person he knows to escape through the sewers. The woman spends the night in Bolek's basement—Izolda is to pick her up early in the morning.

The woman has a "good" look: thick braid, gray eyes, fair skin, and a small nose sprinkled with freckles. They head home. At the first corner they run into a policeman. He looks the women over, grabs the girl by the braid, and pulls her into an entrance. The girl pushes him away, the policeman jostles her against the wall and unbuttons her blouse. Mister, Izolda says in her non-Jewish voice, who do you think you are? Why don't you go out and catch some Jews and leave decent people alone! So?—the policeman turns away from the woman's bust—You want me to go to the workshop in the basement? The sewer guides are still there, Bolek, her husband . . . Shut your mouth, he barks at the girl, but she has no intention of doing so. On the contrary, she starts wailing louder and louder: Let me go, I'm still a virgin . . . The situation is getting unpleasant. People are going to work, they might hear, might get curious . . . Because who shouts "I'm a virgin" at dawn? And who can a policeman shove around inside an entrance like that and get away with it? They could be in for a lot of trouble. Fortunately the policeman is put off by the fact that the girl is a virgin. So he turns to Izolda, and she already knows what to do. She doesn't wail and doesn't struggle. The acquaintance looks discreetly away. The policeman buttons his pants and the two women go home.

The Sweater

Basia and Jurek Gajer are leaving Poland.

The Germans announce that any Jews who are citizens of other countries will be allowed to leave and people buy foreign passports on the black market. Basia and Jurek purchase ones from Honduras and report to the Hotel Polski on Długa Street.

Izolda wants to say goodbye to Basia.

Because it was at her place that she saw a blond man with helpless hands.

Because it was in her apartment that he said: You look like a rabbi's daughter. To which she said: My father is a chemist who's searching for a color that isn't in the rainbow. That's almost the same thing, he said, smiling, and that's how love began.

Izolda wants to catch up before they leave and stays the night with the Gajers. They talk about Honduras, about how they'll have to learn Spanish. That Spanish isn't all that hard. That Basia's colorful sweater will come in handy on the journey. (Basia explains the stitch—which loop goes where—and shows how she tied off all the bits of wool on the inside and covered the knots with a dark pink lining.)

The Germans surround the Hotel Polski at five in the morning. They send everyone to Pawiak prison and separate the Jews from the Poles. Izolda shows her identity card made out to Maria Pawlicka and stays with the Poles who came to say goodbye. Basia and Jurek show their Honduran passports and stay with the Jews. The Germans take the Jews away, the Poles stay in prison. She spends two months in Pawiak.

The Prayer

There are cells on both sides of the corridor. One is for Jewish women. Every day, on her way to the toilet, Izolda steals a glance at them through the spyhole. One morning she notices her husband's mother. She's sitting sideways, resting her chin on her withered, wrinkled hand. That evening she's facing the door, as though she were looking straight at her daughter-in-law.

Izolda shrinks back in a panic.

She returns to her cell.

She asks a new arrival who else the Germans had arrested the day before.

Several people.

Was there a tall young man with straight blond hair?

Yes, there was a man with blond hair.

And how about a dark-haired man with a beard . . . No, what am I saying, without a beard, quite a bit older . . .

Yes, there was a man with dark hair.

And a girl? With bleached yellow hair?

No, no girl.

It's all clear: they caught her husband and his parents, but his sister managed to escape. Izolda struggles not to shout: Listen, everyone, they took my husband! I don't have anyone to live for! But what sense would that make, the women in the cell can't help her, the guards even took away their hairpins. She looks at the others with envy. They wound up here at Pawiak for an important cause, for some act of patriotism. They taught children Polish history or carried secret messages or printed underground leaflets . . . Is it her fault that her only cause is her husband?

For exercise the women are let out into the prison yard.

They totter about, one behind the other, under the eye of the female guard. After a moment five figures appear on the steps—the women from the Jewish cell. Izolda knows—everyone knows—that the Jewish cell is headed into the ruins of the ghetto. Where they will be shot.

Izolda sees her husband's mother.

The Polish women walk four abreast and turn to the left just as the Jewish women pass by, so the two groups are facing each other.

She is frightened.

His mother will recognize her.

His mother will give her away with a look, a gesture . . . Will she smile? Will she say something?

Izolda starts to pray. The way she always does, to the Mother of God on Lilusia's medallion. May she not look in my direction . . . Let her walk past me . . . She breaks out in a sweat, she's wet with fear, she tries speeding up her pace and slowing down . . . The Jewish cell keeps moving across the yard, her own mother-in-law is walking to her death and Izolda is asking the Mother of God to make her step more quickly.

The Jewish women march out of the yard.

The Polish women walk in a circle, in silence, one behind the other.

Shots ring out.

She counts to five.

She thinks: Now it's my husband's turn, now Shayek will be taken out and shot.

The women return to their cell.

The next day someone hands her a smuggled message, from her husband.

The Germans had hauled in a different tall young man with blond hair.

Scorching Hot

The Germans free the women detained at the Hotel Polski.

She goes back home.

She learns from her husband that when the widow learned Izolda was being held at Pawiak she got scared and threw out Shayek's sister and parents. She ordered them to leave at once, in the middle of the day, when the sun was at its peak. And so his parents found themselves on the street, with their "bad" looks and their poor command of Polish—his parents who didn't know the city and who had spent the past six months sitting on the floor.

The day was scorching hot. They must have been blinded by the sun. They looked pale in their heavy dark overcoats—they'd put on their winter clothes before leaving. Like two blind people led by a yellow-haired girl. Shayek's mother believed Halina looked Aryan enough to save herself if she were on her own, and begged her to go: Leave us, please, just walk away, don't stay with us—but Halina didn't want to leave them and the three of them walked on.

They came to the Church of Our Redeemer.

They sat down in a pew. They stayed for several hours, hoping to spend the night there, but someone informed the police. An older man went over to them and whispered: They're waiting for you . . . outside the church . . . Shayek's mother jumped up and dashed onto the street; the policemen chased after her. Halina and her father made it to the courtyard next door.

They took her to Pawiak, her husband explains. Evidently they've already shot her . . .

Yes, she says. They've already shot her.

Did you see her? her husband asks.

Only her back.

Then she corrects herself: First her face, then her back.

She hears her calm, even voice. The voice of her husband when he told her about her father. The voice of the tailors in the ghetto. His mother's gone . . . That's too bad . . . We're still here.

Kangur

Izolda spends a long time at the post office, putting calls in to Krakow for "Mr. Pawlicki." When he picks up she asks what's going on and Mr. Pawlicki reports that yesterday there was a wind off the mountains but today the weather is nice. Or that it's windy today and supposed to be nice tomorrow. This means that everything is in order: her husband met the people in Krakow and escorted them out of the city to meet "Kangur." Kangur will see them to the border, after which some locals will guide them through the Tatras, into Slovakia. The service costs twenty dollars in gold certificates, her husband will receive his share and be able to pay the honest landlady in Śródborów, where Izolda's mother, Halina, and Shayek's father are all living in a gatehouse.

She goes to the post office. Places a call to Krakow. She waits an hour, the operator reports that Mr. Pawlicki doesn't answer, would you like to wait? Two hours pass and still no Mr. Pawlicki.

She tries the next day. No Mr. Pawlicki.

On the third day a man she doesn't recognize answers the phone. Mr. Pawlicki has had an accident, very serious.

She travels to Krakow. The Germans cordoned off the block and took everyone (the man explains), gagged them (she tries to imagine her husband's mouth gagged, she doesn't know what that looks like, she's never seen mouths like that), and bound their feet and legs. The man pays for the tea and whispers: They're still in prison. She whispers back: I see, says goodbye, and goes to the train station.

King of Hearts

The train from Krakow arrives at dawn. Izolda runs straight from the station to Lilusia Szubert's sister

Terenia and immediately starts to explain everything: cordon, gag, prison, Kangur . . . But she doesn't have to. Terenia reaches for a pack of cards: Shuffle them, she says, and cut them with your right hand, toward yourself. Then she lays out the cards and sees everything: a man with blond hair, in love, in other words the king of hearts. See, he's already out the door and on the move. Terenia studies the picture cards and suddenly her voice becomes gleeful: your king has a trip ahead of him, what are you worried about?!

She's right, too: there he is, second row, first card on the right—the king of hearts. Next to him is the six of hearts, which means a trip. Of course those three spades are a bad sign, Terenia explains, but even that's not so tragic: you should be getting news any day now.

She does get news, but it's from Auschwitz, though at least there's an address where she can send packages. On the official postcard her husband writes: "I'm healthy, send something to eat." She sends bread, smoked bacon, onions, one kilogram of sugar, and one of lard. That costs 120 zlotys, she's allowed to send one package per month. Even if I have to die doing it, she tells Lilusia, even if I have to sell myself, I'm going to get that 120 zlotys every month.

Chambre Séparée

She eats her midday meals at the Rose—a restaurant dating from before the war, not elegant perhaps, but respectable. The building was hit by a bomb during the invasion, but the ground floor survived, so the owner cleaned up the debris, replaced the windowpanes, and invited her old patrons back. And they came—professors from the nearby polytechnic and their wives (who now bake cakes at home to sell at the Kiercelak market), as well as the wives of officers currently prisoners in German camps. New customers appear: black marketeers, money changers, smugglers. The owner asks the waiter (not for the first time) to show the new customers a little more courtesy, the waiter assures her that he will try his best.

Izolda shows up at the usual time and takes a seat. Roman the waiter brings dumplings with beetroot and asks if he should bring her husband's meal or are we waiting for him? We're not waiting, she says, my husband's in Auschwitz. And you know what? she adds. I have to get him out.

They give her an extra serving of thick sauce, on the house. Handing Roman her dirty plate, she says: I'll need money. Do you understand? Lots of money . . . She gets up and whispers into his thinning gray hair: I can count on your help, can't I?

A few days later the waiter points to a closed door next to the bar: There . . . he's waiting for you . . . She hesitates: Roman, she whispers . . . Roman shrugs his shoulders: What would you like with your dumplings, beetroot or cabbage?

The room next to the bar looks exactly the way a *chambre séparée* should at a place like the Rose. Discreet lighting, red velvet curtains in the window, a bouquet of dried red roses on a small table, and a slightly worn sofa. A corpulent man is sitting on the sofa, wearing a tight, unbuttoned vest. He's spread his legs, so that his stomach spills over his lap. A perfectly nice older gentleman waiting for a woman.

He asks Izolda to sit down. He moves closer. He lifts her skirt and strokes her thigh. He's moved by the sight of the run in her stocking and promises new ones, real silk.

Do you like me? she asks. If you do, then please, don't buy me anything. Just give me money. I'll do whatever you want, but I need lots of money. You see, my husband is in Auschwitz.

They look at each other. She with her bare thigh and the nice older man with a pinkish, perspiring bald spot. He takes his hand away. Auschwitz, he repeats, in a sad voice . . . He's lost all interest in her stockings and thighs. And I'm going to get him out of there, she adds, fixing her skirt. She smiles nicely and leaves the room. As she passes the waiter she shrugs her shoulders: Unfortunately, Roman, that's not what I meant.

The Jar

Her husband had told her to take the unpaved road from the station and cross through the garden plots in the direction of the mountains. She climbs up the road; the garden plots give way to meadows and gloomy, pitiless trees. On the left should be a large solitary house. And there it is, a pretty wooden house with a veranda all around—the kind of house people from the city built so they could spend their summers with lots of children, a resident aunt making jams and jellies, and artistic friends of questionable health. Izolda hopes it will have a large tiled stove so she can get warm.

The stove is cold. The armchairs are draped with white covers. Evidently Kangur doesn't have consumptive artist friends. He serves her some strong tea. Among the unwashed shot glasses and the remnants of stale bread scattered on the kitchen table, she notices a photograph propped against a silver sugar bowl. The woman in the picture is wearing a fur toque with an embroidered veil; she is heavily made-up and has bright, audacious eyes. He's doing this for her, Izolda thinks, she's the reason Kangur needs the gold dollars. Does she, too, need to get someone out? Izolda studies the woman with envy. Not only does she have eyes like that—she has Kangur.

She tells him in no uncertain terms that she's every bit as capable of shepherding people as her husband. And, if she knew the route through the Tatras . . .

Unfortunately, Kangur won't be taking anyone else and won't be hiring her. He's sorry about the mishap. He can't lend her any money (unfortunately). So there's nothing you can do? she asks. He can give her an address (he jots something on a napkin), but that's all.

The address is for an acquaintance—a Hungarian Jew living in Krakow. The man has a young face and old, tired eyes. He won't lend Izolda any money (unfortunately), but he would be interested in getting his hands on some cyanide. He mentions this very casually, just as she's leaving. A large jar.

In Warsaw she stops in a chemist's shop that she knows from before the war. She used to pass it whenever she went to Pomianowski's bakery, and she always took a moment to look at the display window full of mortars and little bottles and colorful soaps.

The chemist's smells of eau de toilette. She's the only customer. She steps up to the counter and says: I'm interested in potassium cyanide. A large jar.

How soon do you need it? The man at the counter doesn't seem the least bit surprised.

Today.

It'll be tomorrow.

How much does it cost?

Five hundred.

The next day she wonders who's going to be waiting for her: the Gestapo or the Polish police.

The same man is at the counter. He locks the door and hands her a jar wrapped in newspaper. She gives him her mother's ring as security—gold, with a large pale-pink pearl—and takes the train back to Krakow.

How much? asks the Hungarian Jew.

One thousand.

He tells her to come back in the afternoon, he obviously wants to check the goods. The cyanide passes the test and in the evening he pays her one thousand zlotys.

She doesn't ask what he needs the poison for. She presumes it's for other Jews—Polish or Hungarian.

Waiting

She's back in her room at Mrs. Krusiewicz's (she moved from Mariańska Street right after she got out of Pawiak).

Mrs. Krusiewicz works as a seamstress. She is exact, serious, and has principles inherited from her mother, who also sewed for a living.

Izolda has never known a seamstress and sometimes her new landlady's habits surprise her. For instance, every day at two in the afternoon Mr. Krusiewicz closes his shop with religious icons and hangs a sign in the door that says "Closed for lunch" and at two thirty Mrs. Krusiewicz places a soup tureen on the table. Occasionally Mr. Krusiewicz is late and the tureen is sitting there, the soup has turned cold, and Mrs. Krusiewicz refuses to reheat it because the midday meal is served at two thirty.

Izolda finds this strange: she would reheat her husband's soup no matter what the time. And frankly she isn't surprised when one day Mr. Krusiewicz forgoes both his meal and his marriage with Mrs. Krusiewicz and moves out.

The attic apartment is several flights up. The staircase is dark and gloomy. When Izolda is out, Mrs. Krusiewicz leaves a lit candle next to the door. When Izolda comes back she sees the tiny flicker of light and feels safer. At least someone in this world is watching out for her.

Her husband's letters come to her old address, so she goes to Mariańska Street and asks Mateusz the caretaker if there's any word. Bad news, Mrs. Pawlicka, he says, something's wrong, a package came back from Auschwitz.

Throwing up into a public bin, she thinks: At least I know where to buy the white powder. She wipes her mouth and returns home. She takes the candle from the hall and places it on the table in front of her like a graveside votive. Then she slumps over the table, her arms wrapped around the package. Mrs. Krusiewicz carefully pulls the package out from under her head. The gray paper is full of stamps and crossed-out words in German. Mrs. Krusiewicz studies the writing. *Neue Adresse abwarten*, she reads out loud. Wait for new address . . . Wait! she cries out. You see? You just have to wait!

Ice Cream

Izolda has plenty of free time. She doesn't send packages. She doesn't try to get money. She doesn't buy sugar, onions, bacon, or bread. She doesn't have to get out of bed and get dressed. She doesn't even have to wake up.

At times—mostly just before daybreak—she's convinced that *Neue Adresse abwarten* is a hoax. They say to wait but there won't be any new address. He's dead. Either they've killed him or he's died of hunger, typhus, tuberculosis, exhaustion . . . She repeats the word "dead," spelling it out: d-e-a-d. Then she adds her husband: m-y-h-u-s-b-a-n-d-i-s-d-e-a-d.

Mrs. Krusiewicz begs her to get out of bed. What for? she asks. Mrs. Krusiewicz reminds her that she was supposed to take her husband's suit to the dry cleaner's. What for? she asks. All right, then just go out for a walk.

She doesn't want to upset Mrs. Krusiewicz so she goes out for a walk. She passes an ice-cream shop. The doors are open and a young couple is walking out, each holding a flat wafer with ice cream on top. She imagines that they're she and her husband, walking down the street eating ice cream. But in cones, like her husband preferred.

There are different ways to eat ice cream from a cone.

You can lick around the edges. You can put the whole thing in your mouth. You can bite off tiny pieces, starting at the top. You can go slow or fast, and if you slow down, the ice cream melts and runs down in a sticky streak between your fingers.

How did her husband eat his ice cream?

Did he lick around the edges?

Did he start at the top?

Slow or fast?

She doesn't remember.

She goes back to the shop and buys one scoop, and tries out different ways. It's horrible: she can't remember how her husband ate ice cream!

She gives up on her walk. She boards a tram—and there's another couple, sitting right across from her. They don't look at each other, don't talk, the man rests his hand on the woman's lap. The woman adjusts her coat and removes his hand, he puts it back, without looking.

Izolda feels a strange sensation.

Not her, but her knee.

Her knee is yearning for a hand.

Not Izolda, only her knee. Her knee has become a separate living, yearning creature.

She looks at the man's hand, but that's not the hand her knee is after.

She sighs with relief: she doesn't remember how he ate his ice cream, but her knee remembers his hand.

Worse

She prefers the tram to walking because in the tram she's less outside, less exposed. The most outside are windows on the ground floor. She can see the people inside—how they're talking, carrying a glass of tea, or watering flowers in a pot. She knows that they, too, have their worries: Lilusia assures her that these days every Polish household has its share of suffering. She believes Lilusia, but she also knows very well that Polish suffering is better, even enviable.

Her suffering is worse, because she is worse. That's what the whole world thinks, and the whole world can't be wrong when it comes to a sense of good and bad, or rather, better and worse.

She is worse and that's why she is in disguise. She has a new name and a new hair color and a new voice and laugh and a new way of carrying her handbag. And she prefers her new self to the real thing. So what does that mean?

That her disguised self . . . that her pretend self is better than her real self.

A Night

Your king has a trip ahead . . . the king of hearts is thinking about you . . . (Terenia taps on the king and the ace of hearts. There, look: he's thinking. Of course he's alive, otherwise he wouldn't be thinking.) The trip will end well and there'll be a meeting. A meeting with a sad man. A man with auburn hair. I think I know who it is, Terenia cries out: I read cards for his fiancée. The cards said that someone would be locked up and look, they sent her off to Ravensbrück. Maybe we should pay him a visit? You're sad, he's sad . . .

They visit the sad man with auburn hair, gray eyes, and dark, bushy eyebrows. He serves them cherry liqueur and sausage from Karczew. The man is a lyrical tenor and hums Nadir's aria from *The Pearl Fishers*, he even sings in French: *Je crois entendre encore—lala-lala-lala—sa voix tendre et sonore* (at "his voice, tender and sonorous" Izolda starts to cry). He tells them about studying with Didur. Adam Didur, you've heard of him, haven't you?

Terenia takes her leave and the sad host moves a little closer.

He likes her hair.

(That's not my real hair, mine is darker.)

He likes her name.

(That's not my real name . . .)

Is there anything real about you? he asks.

Waiting. That's the most real thing about me.

The sad man assures her that he knows all about waiting, too, and puts his arm around her.

That's not the neck his arm is yearning for, she thinks, and he'll realize that in a moment.

She's not wrong: the sad man removes his hand. He sighs. He whispers soothingly to cheer her up: You'll get a new address, you'll send him a package . . . What will you send?

Izolda lets herself daydream: Onions, garlic, smoked bacon, maybe sugar . . .

Bacon? The man brightens up. Where do you buy that?

At the Kiercelak market, behind where they sell white bread, in a booth with a little awning.

I wonder if my wife would eat smoked bacon, thinks the tenor, she was always so picky.

Then buy the raw bacon. It's just as nutritious, and cheaper.

He strokes her hand . . . My neighbor waited and waited, and look, yesterday she got a message. Smuggled out of the camp at Skarżysko-Kamienna.

They don't speak. It gets dark—curfew hour. They light a carbide lamp. In the morning she asks him: How did that message get to your neighbor?

The usual way, somebody brought it. A man by the name of Franciszek.

For free?

Her host is surprised at the question: Who carries messages these days for free?!

The Deal

She tracks down the man by the name of Franciszek (the sad tenor's neighbor told her where to look) in a workers' colony. The two-story building houses several apartments and is surrounded by pine trees (an empty hammock is strung between two of the trunks). She tells Franciszek who sent her. She praises the collection of Gypsy dolls displayed on fluffy embroidered cushions. She admires the numerous trophies set out on the cabinet, asks him about the fishing competitions and whether he doesn't need couriers for delivering messages. He does. Mr. Franciszek works in the Hasag factory together with Jews from the camp and takes letters from them to their families. He delivers them himself if he has time, and if he doesn't he hands them over to people he trusts. For each letter delivered the trusted person receives ten zlotys. She doesn't ask Mr. Franciszek how much the Jews pay him. She agrees to the ten zlotys and he gives her several little notes. All are written in small letters and, according to Mr. Franciszek, all say the same thing: Sell something. A fur collar, a tablecloth, a ladle, anything—and send money by the same route. And if there's nothing to sell, then borrow from the cousins. And if there aren't any cousins, then say hello to whoever is left.

She stashes the letters in her bra and asks where she can buy fatback bacon.

She travels out to the country, buys fatback, and sells it at Kiercelak. She delivers the messages, takes the replies back to Franciszek, and he pays her ten zlotys for each one. She hides another batch in her bra and travels out to the country.

You mean you're taking money for delivering messages? Lilusia is taken aback.

She understands her friend's honorable attitude and her surprise, but Izolda unfortunately can't afford to do anything for free. She has to pay for the gatehouse at Śródborów. She has to get her husband out of the camp as soon as she finds out where he is. She isn't doing anything for free and doesn't feel the least bit guilty.

The Doctor

She's supposed to meet a man they call "the Doctor." She doesn't know him. He's an acquaintance of Sonia Landau (Izolda barely knows her). Shayek's sisters were friends with Sonia and little Szymuś was very fond of her. Szymuś always went to Sonia when he quarreled with his girlfriend Anula. They used to squabble over building blocks: little Anula insisted on building a wall, Szymuś preferred a tree. We have to have a forest, he said, because we have to have Józefów, but Anula knocked all the blocks down. I'm a gendarme, she shouted, and you're a smuggler, bang—well, fall down, can't you see I'm shooting at you? And once again Szymuś went running to Sonia Landau: Tell her there's no shooting in Józefów!

Szymuś is gone, the sisters are gone. Sonia is still here and knows of a Gestapo officer who's said to be a decent man. When a friend is arrested she telephones Gestapo headquarters on Szucha Avenue, but a different officer answers. He would be happy to stand in for his colleague, how can he be of help? Sonia explains how her friend was arrested. The officer expresses his sympathy and invites her to coffee. Sonia tells him she'll be wearing a dark blue skirt with a red blouse, he'll have no problem recognizing her. And she's right: he has no problem recognizing her, he pulls her into the car and takes her to Pawiak prison.

The Doctor rides up on a bicycle—he's wearing knickerbockers and a cycling cap. He's in tears because he was in love with Sonia Landau. Slowly he collects himself and asks about Izolda's husband. He'll try to help, since Sonia asked him to. He says he'll arrange for Shayek to be sent to Warsaw (but that's going to cost) and will see that he gets released (which will cost even more).

She thanks the Doctor effusively and gives him everything: the money she made from the fatback bacon and the smuggled messages, the laundry receipt for her husband's suit, and letters to all the friends who are looking after her belongings. Each letter has the same six words: "Please give the Doctor everything—Izolda." (She signs as Izolda and not Marynia so it's more genuine.) Even if she's arrested, she tells the Doctor, he should collect all her things, sell them, and save her husband. Not her, only her husband, do you understand? I understand, he says gravely, and stashes away the money and the letters.

The next day Lilusia asks her why she's sending a complete stranger. Terenia asks as well (she gave the man what he asked for; after all, he had a letter). And Mrs. Krusiewicz did the same. Even the cleaners handed him her husband's suit (made of English wool with a blue check, he looked so handsome, so elegant wearing that suit . . .). Is there something wrong? the owner of the laundry asks, concerned. No, everything's all right, she assures him, then goes onto the street and bursts into desperate, helpless tears.

Armchair. Stockings

Shortly after the war she decided to pay the Doctor a visit. I'm going to walk in, she told herself, say hello and tell him . . .

On her way there she planned what to say.

"I risked my life to earn a few pennies, and you . . ."

That's not it. What does he care about her life . . .

"What did you think, that you'd get God knows what: dollars, jewelry? And all you wound up with was a few towels and some sheets. And a beach robe."

(She was moved, remembering that robe. It was yellow, soft, with a large white collar. She wore it at the beach. She'd just come in from the water. The beach was in Sopot. She went there with her father . . .)

Not that either. Better not say anything, just ask him . . .

The Doctor opened the door.

He stepped back, surprised: Is it really you? And he was happy, truly happy. That she had survived. And your husband? He shouted with joy: That's wonderful!

He asked her to tell him all about it, one thing at a time. He listened excitedly and only interrupted once, when she was talking about Auschwitz. He asked if she'd run into Sonia Landau there. She had, Sonia had given her some warm stockings. And a towel. She worked in the *Effektenkammer* . . . He didn't understand: Where did she work? In an office. She was assigned to Canada, where she organized the belongings left by the Hungarian Jews. Used, but still very good quality, very respectable. The Doctor didn't understand what she meant by Canada or what happened to the Hungarian Jews. She didn't want to explain. She no longer wanted to ask him anything. She said goodbye. She went down Marszałkowska Street and turned onto one of the side streets—Hoża or Wspólna, she couldn't tell since everything was in ruins. It was getting dark. In the distance she could see a square and what was probably Ujazdowskie Avenue. It already had a new name. Excuse me, is that Stalin Avenue? she asked a passerby. The man stopped, took out a lighter, and shone it on her face. MY DEAR LADY, he said, overaccentuating every word, THAT WAS, IS, AND WILL BE—WILL BE, MY DEAR LADY—UJAZDOWSKIE AVENUE. She was ashamed, thanked him, and kept on walking.

Hail Mary

She takes the train to get more messages, more fatback bacon.

A German railway officer enters her compartment and asks for her travel permit. She doesn't have one, so she hands him her identity card and one hundred zlotys, like everyone else who travels without a permit. The officer is supposed to tuck away the one hundred zlotys, return the ID, and leave—that's what they've all done before. This one doesn't tuck anything away. He doesn't return her ID. He stares at her, stares at her photograph, and finally says: *Kommen Sie mit*—and gestures toward the rear of the car.

When the train stops in Radom the German takes her to the police station.

Evidently you look like a Jew, says the policeman.

She's genuinely surprised: I look like a Jew? I've never heard that before.

Can you say your Hail Mary? the policeman asks.

Of course. *Hail Mary, full of grace, the Lord is with thee* . . . (Lilusia taught her when she put the necklace on Izolda: Repeat after me, she said . . .) *Blessed art thou among women* . . . Because she is addressing the Mother of God, who is full of grace, she goes slowly, making every word count, to show respect.

Listen to you, the policeman laughs out loud. What normal person says Hail Mary like that? Usually it's hail-maryfullofgracethelordiswiththee . . . You really are a Jew!

Apparently Lilusia forgot the most important thing: that the delivery has to sound completely ordinary. Poor Lilusia—she thought about handbags and medallions, but it never occurred to her there might be a Jewish way of saying the Hail Mary.

Izolda spends the night in a solitary cell. She repeats the Hail Mary out loud (she doesn't know if she's praying or just learning to say it like a normal person). The next morning a policeman comes for her.

The Radom Gestapo looks like any other office. The windows don't have curtains, the desks are small and in need of repair, each one seats two men facing each other. They pore over their papers, paying no attention to her, so she sits down on the doorstep. (Is that how a Jewish woman sits? she wonders. Would she stretch her legs out in such a casual way? Certainly not. A Jewish woman would just stand there like a stone, resigned, with despair in her eyes.)

A Gestapo officer comes in carrying a small object wrapped in paper.

He beckons her over.

The man opens a drawer, takes out a white place-mat, and spreads it on his desk, unwraps the paper . . . He's brought a loaf of expertly braided challah, nicely browned, with a crumb topping—genuine Jewish challah! She quickly looks away from the bread and stares at the Gestapo officer. (Would a Jew stare that way? So calmly, or even perhaps confidently?) The Gestapo man breaks off a piece of challah with one hand and slaps her with the other. He doesn't hit her hard. It's a short, precise blow just to say: You will not stare at me—nothing more.

Going to get some bacon, weren't you? the Gestapo man guesses.

She protests vigorously (for selling fatback you could be sent to a concentration camp) and opens her handbag. She takes out her papers, her mirror, her comb—and a letter she was delivering to Franciszek.

The letter reports on the family's health and ends with the most important thing: "Be calm, I've made sure the child is in good hands . . ." The Gestapo man sends for a translator. A balding, nondescript civilian with hunched shoulders scans the letter. He stops at the last sentence. He hesitates a moment . . . He begins to translate. He speaks very slowly and deliberately: Uncle's broken leg is healing well . . . No, healing isn't right, Uncle's broken leg is knitting back together nicely . . . I visited Grandmama and Grandpapa, they both have rheumatism . . . The Gestapo officer is getting bored. He interrupts the translator and signals: Take her away.

The Whole World

There are twenty-five women in the Radom jail cell. They begin the day cleaning. They scrub the floor with a brush, mop up the water with a rag, and wring the rag out over a bucket. When it's her turn the water spills onto the floor and runs down her sleeves . . . Twenty-four women, poor and wealthy alike, look at her in amazement. They look at her that way because they scrub quickly and expertly and no one pays any attention to them.

When she was fourteen a servant girl used to carry her satchel to school. And once she was back home, Izolda would lift her right leg and then her left and the servant girl would bend over to pull off her dirty snow boots. Izolda was a very nice little girl, except she didn't carry her own satchel and didn't pull off her own boots.

She stops to think: Who helped the wealthy women in her cell take their shoes off, when they were fourteen? And why is it that a wealthy Polish woman knows how to mop the floor and a wealthy Jewish woman doesn't?

She'd like to discuss the matter with her husband.

The thought of her husband makes her heart ache so much she feels it will explode.

She breaks into tears, and the woman from the next bunk gives her a scolding look. You're crying over a fellow, aren't you? I can bet it's not for your mother. Now listen here and don't forget: you can have as many fellows as you'd like, but you only have one mother . . .

I know, she agrees, I only have one mother, but as far as I'm concerned the whole world can fall apart or go up in flames or disappear—just as long as he stays alive.

Pfui, what are you going on about . . . the woman from the next bunk is disgusted. Go up in flames? The whole world? *Pfui!*

Ingeborg

The Poles stand in one long, silent, and dismal row while the German farmers pass back and forth in front of them, looking them over, pawing and squeezing their shoulders, their necks, their hands, their legs. Finally they point and say: That man there. Or else: That woman.

A tall, thin woman steps up to Izolda. Her hair is pinned in a small bun, her brow is penciled black. She tests Izolda's shoulders, which are in order, and inspects her palms, which are large. All in all Izolda is a tall, sturdy woman, and the German points at her.

A female clerk standing behind the farmers writes down in her notebook: Maria Pawlicka, Raddusch. Then she smiles kindly at Izolda and says: Good luck.

Raddusch is a village with respectable houses, a train station, and a POW camp. The German woman takes her to a room with an earth floor where another forced laborer is already living. He comes from around Kielce and his name is Józio.

Evening comes. Izolda lies down on the straw mattress and tries to fall asleep. In the darkness she hears bare feet and Józio whispering: Move over. She takes him by the arm. Józio, she says gently, I'm married, my husband is in a camp, and you're a good Pole, right? So go back to your bed.

Józio proves to be a good Pole, but he feels sad. He wants her to cheer him up, talk to him, tell him a story, but it has to be interesting . . . She doesn't know any interesting stories. Of course you do, he insists. Just think of something.

She's got it: High above the city, on a tall column, stood the statue of the Happy Prince . . .

Józio doesn't like fairy tales. He wants to hear something real, most of all something about love.

I'll tell you about a girl, she begins. She had green eyes and ventured out of the depths of the forest to visit her lover, always at daybreak . . .

And so she recounts the story of Ingeborg, her and Hala Borensztajn's favorite book. The summer was hot that year and the earth was on fire, as though someone had baked bread on the very ground. The sunlight was hot, too . . .

Sunlight at daybreak isn't hot, Józio corrects. And the earth can't be on fire, especially in the forest.

Don't interrupt, she says. They felt like they were on fire, so that's how the earth felt, too.

Izolda and Hala were always very envious of that Ingeborg. Not over Axel—he would have been much too old for them—but because he loved her so much. On the way home from school they promised each other that neither would get married unless they found a love like that.

We made a promise . . . she tells Józio.

Who's we?

Hala Boren . . . my friend Hala and I.

And did you wait? asks Józio.

I waited.

And your friend?

What about my friend?

Are you listening to me? Is your friend still waiting?

She's still waiting, Józio. Now go to sleep.

The farmer's wife wakes her up in the morning and sends her to the cowshed to milk the cows. Izolda has never seen cows up close. The farmer's wife watches her trying to take the udder, then sends her to help with the threshing instead. Izolda has never seen a thresher before either. The German woman tells her to sweep the bits of straw off the machine, watches her, and sends her back to the cowshed, where a cow knocks out one of her front teeth. So she's sent to the washroom. Izolda has seen a tub and washboard before: their servant girl used them. She sits down to use the washboard . . . What do you know how to do? asks the German woman. I know how to take care of people who are sick. (She almost blurts out: Sick with typhus.) Nobody's sick here, everyone's healthy. The German woman is getting annoyed. And what else? Izolda thinks for a moment. I'm pretty good at French . . . The German woman starts to yell and sends her back to the thresher.

Charmante

The news that Izolda speaks French makes its way to the POW camp.

An officer stops in for a visit. His uniform is dirty and marked with white letters: KG for *Kriegsgefangener*—prisoner of war. He's longing to talk to a charming woman, *avec une femme charmante.* He bows and kisses her hand.

She smiles to the officer as winsomely as she can with a missing front tooth. She tries to recall what charming women talk about with handsome men. Not about typhus. Not about Pawiak. Not about packages to Auschwitz either . . . The Frenchman calls her his little girl, *ma petite.* It would be good to know what little girls talk about. The war will end and then what? She won't know how to talk with a man?

Factory

The farmer's wife is fed up with her milking, laundering, threshing, and French and sends her to the labor bureau. She's reassigned to a canvas mill, where she works alongside German women. They tend the looms, fixing any broken threads. There are several hundred looms in the hall, the women run from thread to thread. They're deaf from all the noise, they have varicose veins on their legs and white dust in their hair, eyelashes, and brows . . . They aren't good to her. They aren't bad to her. They are tired. She asks how long they've been running from thread to thread. Fifteen years. Twenty . . . My God, she says, shocked, but the German women cheer her up: You'll get used to it.

A Walk

They don't work Sundays and are allowed to go into town on a pass. The French POW receives a pass as well, he borrows a civilian jacket, drapes it over the KG sewn on his coat, and they go for a walk.

The city is called Cottbus. They see men on crutches and haggard, badly dressed women . . . An air-raid siren goes off. They take shelter in an entrance. I'm here, the Frenchman whispers, and shields her with his manly arm, to protect her from the bombs. Panes go flying out of the windows, his words get drowned out by the shattering glass. The planes quieten down one minute and come back the next, like a storm unable to pass. It reminds her of the air raid in Warsaw and the garrison church.

There was this priest who asked me to pray for him, she tells the Frenchman.

And?

Nothing. I didn't do it.

Not once? That's not nice, the Frenchman scolds. Not nice at all . . .

She tries to explain as she walks him to the station: I'm saving all my prayers for one person, I don't have strength to pray for anyone else. Do you understand?

Of course he does, *ça se comprend.*

The Frenchman goes back to Raddusch.

An idea hits her and she looks around the station for a train schedule. It's easy to travel from Raddusch to Cottbus and from there to Łódź, renamed Litzmannstadt.

The Coat

They don't work Sundays . . . No one checks to see if they're there . . . That means that all Sunday long no one will be looking for her . . .

Saturday evening she takes the local train to Raddusch.

She plans to spend the night at Józio's and leave in the morning. The bed in the little room is occupied, but Józio has important information: he has an aunt in Łódź. Go to Nawrot Street, he says, find the linen press and tell my aunt that I say hello. And give her this (he reaches under his straw mattress and takes out a matchbox containing an oval stone he passed in his urine, in great pain because of his ailing kidney). What's this for? A present. A keepsake.

The Frenchman smuggles her inside the POW camp and takes her to the shower room. She can sleep there since it isn't used at night. He spreads his coat on the floor. He brings her an envelope and a sheet of paper. She sits on the coat—the floor reeks of soapsuds and Lysol—and writes a letter.

The Frenchman asks who she's writing to.

My friend Stefa.

Is she pretty? asks the Frenchman.

She has pretty dark blue eyes, with long lashes.

(Stefa had a grandmother from Vienna, a crazy mother who ran off with a younger man, and a father who was bitter and not good at much. They rented out rooms. When they didn't have lodgers, Stefa couldn't afford textbooks or school trips. Izolda very much wanted to help and collected money from friends or sold film tickets at school. So Stefa went on the trip to Wieliczka, but didn't even give Izolda so much as a crib for the algebra test.

I didn't have time—she explained—I barely managed to finish myself.) Thanks to her Viennese grandmother, Stefa is fluent in German and works at the offices of the Ostbahn railway. She has a locked drawer where she can keep valuables. Izolda left her silver compact there every time she went to see Franciszek.

Sitting on a coat in the shower room of the French prisoners, she tells her friend that she's been sick lately. "I don't know if we'll meet again. If we don't, give the compact to my husband. If you don't see my husband, keep it for yourself. I hope it brings you luck."

The Frenchman looks over her shoulder and asks what she's writing about to her pretty friend.

About a compact.

The Frenchman is enchanted by her handwriting, by her hand that's holding the pencil, by her knee that's holding the paper, by her dusky, silken skin . . .

She gets up, undresses, stands under the shower. She turns on the warm water and washes her neck, her breasts, her thighs, her stomach . . . Here she has no disguise. And here she is no worse than anyone else. She's not Jewish, not Polish. And she's prettier than the women who haven't had teeth knocked out, who don't get dragged out of rickshaws or shoved into an entrance at dawn.

Early in the morning they go to the station. She asks the Frenchman to post the letter. He begs her to make it through the war. Promise that you will, he says, and he starts to cry. It's nice that she isn't expected to save that Frenchman, that she's the one who's supposed to survive.

She climbs aboard the train.

She doesn't try to remember the French name or the address in Provence.

She has to make a decision: Do I take a seat in the compartment? Stand in the corridor? Hide in the toilet?

The Aunt

On Nawrot Street the caretaker whistles as he clears the snow with a shovel. A child is building a snowman. The linen press is open, Józio's aunt carefully removes the sheets from the rollers and folds them. She looks at the kidney stone, moved, and invites Izolda to spend the night at the press.

Józio's aunt is officially in the Reich, Warsaw is in the *Generalgouvernement*. The border isn't far, you just take the number 12 tram, make your way to Stryków, and find someone to take you across. Everybody knows who they are: they trade sugar for stockings and vodka for warm underwear, or else sugar for warm underwear.

Józio's aunt generously gives Izolda some socks for the smugglers and a pair of stockings for her, with a long black arrow pattern. She assures Izolda that arrows are the latest fashion, they start above the ankle and have to be darker than the stocking.

Armchair. More Urgent Matters

One year she will say: I have to look them up. I have to thank Mr. Bolek, who led me through the sewers; Józio's aunt, who gave me presents; the woman in Stryków who cooked dumplings; the German family in Berlin . . .

A few more years will pass and she will say: It really is high time I pay them a visit. Mr. Bolek. Józio's aunt. The woman in Stryków . . .

She won't visit anyone. Not that she was ungrateful, on the contrary—she will think about them time and time again. That's just how it will work out, because there will always be more urgent matters that need attention.

Number 12 Tram

She takes the tram. She reads the German names of the streets and tries to guess (she doesn't know why) what they used to be called. The tram comes to some barbed wire and slows down. There's a guard post and behind it a bearded man wearing a yellow patch on his overcoat. The patch is in tatters, in the shape of a star. In Warsaw they had different stars—blue, on armbands. Seconds later it dawns on her: that man is a Jew. This is the ghetto. She didn't realize that number 12 went through the ghetto. A few passersby stop and peer inside the tram. She's sitting by the window and they fix their gaze on her, on no one else but her. She turns away, but there are people on the other side as well. They just stand there stony-faced, peering inside . . .

At the end of the line she gets off together with a young woman her own age. She tells the woman about the forced labor and her escape, the woman invites her home. The woman's mother is very kind, makes her feel welcome. What do you like, she asks Izolda, dumplings? The mother cooks a pot of dumplings especially for her and mixes in some cracklings: Eat up, she encourages Izolda, for your health. Well, here things aren't so sweet for us either, she explains that evening. Business used to be better, the gendarmes were fewer, and now they're searching everywhere for Jews. They're looking for Jews and finding all the goods. Eat, child, for your health. They make her bed, cover her with a down duvet, and wake her in the middle of the night: the smugglers are here.

The men look tired and dirty, a little like Bolek's crew. They take vodka and sugar out of their rucksacks and pack women's underwear. Izolda trades the socks from Józio's aunt for a white sheet. They give her instructions: we hold the sheet over our head, we move by jumping, and every few meters we crouch down. Then we keep still for a while. Make sure you're covered by the sheet, it has to touch the snow. Please remember: keep absolutely still. Then we take a few more jumps and crouch down again. We call it rabbit hopping, think you can manage?

She runs with the men—across the snow-covered field, through the forest, across another field—she crouches, doesn't take off the sheet, keeps absolutely still, then runs again. A pale, cold sun appears. They're in the *Generalgouvernement*. She hands back her sheet and asks the way to the nearest train station.

Joy

She dyes her hair (her favorite color—ash blond).

She replaces her tooth (the new tooth comes on a little screw, very practical, the technician assured her, you can take it out if you need to. She found that strange: why would you want to take out an artificial tooth?).

She retrieves her compact. (Stefa cried so much when she received your letter, says Stefa's colleague, a typist at the Ostbahn. She was so sorry she didn't give you that crib for algebra . . . But I'm giving you a hat instead, Stefa announces, and sure enough she hands Izolda a beautiful black hat, with a large fancy brim, a keepsake from her romantic mother.) The typist gives her a pair of patent-leather shoes with high heels (custom-made on Nowy Świat right before the war) and Mrs. Krusiewicz painstakingly alters the overcoat left by her husband.

Izolda stands on the corner of Piękna Street, waiting for her acquaintance, an excellent translator of German poetry (the excellent translator is supposed to find a buyer for the pearl ring—if the price isn't exorbitant).

She's cold and stamps on the wet snow.

Wearing the patent-leather shoes from the machinist.

Wearing the romantic hat from Stefa.

Wearing the silk stockings with the black arrow print from Józio's aunt.

Wearing the overcoat from Mr. Krusiewicz.

Two women wearing civilian dress look her over and come up to her. Waiting for someone? one of them asks, her hands in a fur muff. May I see your identity card? She takes a police badge out of her muff. I don't understand . . . Izolda says in a very sweet, pleading voice, why are you asking? Just don't pretend, says the other. And don't smile. You're all alike, first all innocent smiles and then nothing but tears. Let's go.

She follows the policewoman.

The nearest station is on Poznańska Street. Not a good place, getting out won't be easy.

She has her pearl ring. She thinks: Should I give it to her right away? And why did she say you're all alike? By all she means Jews. Excuse me, ma'am, she risks the question. What did you mean by all alike? Stop playing dumb—the policewoman now makes no effort to be polite. I'm from the vice squad, now do you understand?

Now she understands.

They're not taking her for a Jew but for a whore. What a relief, thank God, they're just taking me for a whore.

She now walks more lightly, like any other woman genuinely amused at such a preposterous idea.

The policewoman sits at a little desk, unfolds the identity card, and reads out loud. So you're married, well, well. And where is your husband passing the time?

She says: He's passing the time in a camp. He was in Auschwitz.

You aren't lying? The policewoman looks up from the desk and changes her tone: Are you sure that's true?

My husband is in a camp, she repeats. I have a letter . . .

The policewoman gets up, as if she intended to escort her to the door. I'm going to check everything, she says sternly. You can go, but I'm going to check . . . And you better . . . she pauses for a moment. Couldn't you make an effort to dress more decently?

Armchair. Everything in Life

If she hadn't been loitering on the street so absurdly dressed, she wouldn't have been taken for a prostitute.

If the policewoman hadn't sent her away, she wouldn't have stopped in on Mariańska Street to see Mateusz the caretaker.

If she hadn't visited Mateusz (she wanted to warn him that the vice squad would be enquiring about her), she wouldn't have learned that the postman had been there.

That he had delivered a letter.

That her husband was asking for food. And that he had sent a new address: Mauthausen, Block AKZ.

In short, everything in life is interwoven in enigmatic ways.

Enough

Shayek's father and sister will stay in Józefów—Lilusia rented them a room in one of the summer houses from before the war. Izolda looks around, moved. Nothing has changed, except the hedge has grown . . . 115 centimeters, according to the owner, that's twenty-three centimeters a year. I'm waiting for my husband to trim it when he comes back.

(What are they talking about?—Halina's father doesn't hear well.

That the war's been going on for five years, Halina explains.

Are they saying how long it will last?

No, Papa, but I'm sure it won't be over anytime soon . . .)

The room is sunny, the air outside is healthy, but Halina keeps saying she's had enough.

I've had enough, she tells the owner.

As you wish, the woman replies, but Captain Szubert's wife paid in advance.

I'm very grateful to you, she tells Lilusia, you've been so generous, it's just that I've had enough.

Halina travels to Warsaw. Without any reason; she simply wants to go, and so she does. She keeps saying: I'm fine, really, I'm doing very well, except . . .

You have to stick it out, Izolda tells her. Here you have fresh air, no one pays any attention to you . . .

No one? Halina smiles. But someone is paying attention, you see. That's right, a man. He's very nice but not very young. We understand each other . . . Halina smiles again, somewhat secretively. We understand each other without words . . .

That makes Izolda nervous.

Halina isn't as tall or pretty as her sisters, her legs aren't very attractive, and her hair is a uniform bleached yellow from the peroxide. Who would be interested in her? Izolda has a bad feeling, but Lilusia isn't worried. Good that she has a man, things will be easier for her.

Lilusia rides out to Józefów to pay the next rent. The owner is surprised: Miss Halina isn't here anymore. Nor is the older gentleman. How should I know where they are? They went away.

They've gone, Lilusia says when she comes back. The landlady thought I knew all about it. Some man came, the landlady hadn't seen him before, but it was clear that Halina knew him. He helped them pack up and put her rucksack on his shoulder. They took the path through the woods, toward the tracks. The man with the rucksack, Halina with the flowers, and her father.

With flowers?

Yes, a small bouquet. The man had brought them. Early spring flowers, probably from the florist. A modest bouquet, but from the florist, the landlady says. She didn't know anything more, Lilusia adds. They left and that was all. With an older man. About a month ago.

The Plaid Blanket

She has a great idea: she'll go to Vienna. Why are you looking at me like that? she asks Lilusia. He's in Mauthausen, isn't he? In other words, Austria. In Vienna I'll be closer and it will be easier for me to get him out, am I right? You're right, dear, Lilusia agrees, with the soothing kind of smile a healthy person uses when speaking to a lunatic. Why shouldn't you go to Vienna? Go there and find him.

But Lilusia doesn't know how to get to Vienna.

Terenia sees an office clerk next to the queen of hearts, but the cards don't say where to find him.

Vienna . . . my God . . . the sad tenor is visibly moved. Zosia and I saw *The Barber of Seville* there. Izolda cuts him off after the first few measures and promises to listen to the entire cavatina when she returns.

She goes to see Stefa. Then the chemist with cyanide. Franciszek in Skarżysko. Kangur near the Slovak border. The Hungarian Jew in Krakow. Roman the waiter at the Rose. My husband's in Mauthausen, she explains to each, it will be easier to get him out if I'm in Vienna, can you tell me how I can travel to Austria? My husband's in Mauthausen . . .

Mrs. Krusiewicz sends her to a woman for whom she used to sew bed linen. The woman's husband was a judge, she now runs a nursery school (and will take in Jewish children for limited stays).

Outside it's cold and dark. The judge's wife is lying sick in her wide double bed, with a lamp on the nightstand and a glass of tea. Her legs are covered with a plaid blanket. Soft and fluffy, with a colorful check pattern.

The judge offers Izolda tea with a slice of lemon, then fixes his wife's pillow. After that he adjusts her plaid blanket, carefully and tenderly wrapping it around her legs to keep out any draughts.

The judge doesn't have the faintest idea how to reach Vienna. Izolda responds: What a nice plaid blanket. It must be very warm . . . And it's light, isn't it? So light and at the same time so warm . . . It's a plaid blanket like any other, the judge is puzzled. Where did we buy it, dear?

She rises from the chair, takes a biscuit for the road, wishes a speedy recovery, and promises to greet Mrs. Krusiewicz.

Closer

Viennese children are running to school with their satchels, Viennese bakers are carrying trays of rolls, the cafés are pouring genuine mocha, and the restaurants are serving Viennese breakfast. Except you need a ration card to buy a sausage. The waiters cut out the coupons with small, elegant scissors that dangle on chains from their belts. If need be, ration cards may be acquired on the black market at Mexikoplatz. The waiter at the Sacher recommends their famous cake and patiently explains to the regulars that there's a legal battle over the name "Sachertorte" but he personally has no doubt the court will award exclusive rights to the hotel.

In the evening it becomes clear a war is on. Windows are covered and streets are dark. People have flashlights. There was a shortage of batteries and someone invented a flashlight activated by a button. The buttons give off a high-pitched, penetrating noise, which resonates in the darkness, and that's how you can tell Vienna is at war.

(She travels to Vienna on an excellent pass, thanks to the waiter at the Rose, who had introduced her to one of the new clients held in special esteem by the owner. The man was completely gray and very short, a full head shorter than Izolda. She was quick to sit down so he wouldn't feel bad, but he wasn't at all self-conscious. He didn't let them take his hat off the hook—he stopped the waiter's hand, then quickly jumped up and grabbed his hat. She laughed. He gave her a stern look; she was scared she had offended him, and didn't say a word. The gray-haired man arranged for her to meet a German he did business with, an engineer from the Todt Organization, which built military barracks, bridges, and roads—and issued work papers as well as travel permits. The engineer in Warsaw told Izolda that his colleague in Vienna would give her the address of her assignment. Assuming you want to work for us . . . the engineer began. Of course she wanted to, and he issued her a *Marschbefehl*. The engineer didn't want money, he preferred tobacco, ten kilos, whole-leaf only.

She packed the tobacco leaves in a black lacquered suitcase, covered them with a nightdress, and set off for Vienna. The engineer's sister—nice part of town, the first *Bezirk*, marble staircase, Bechstein piano in the salon—carefully counted out the notes. Half of what they would have paid at Mexikoplatz, but still nothing to sneeze at. And in addition she told Izolda where to buy Italian silk, fashionable but inexpensive.

In the Todt office near Karl-Lueger-Platz, the engineer's Viennese colleague offered her a job in Dalmatia. Since Dalmatia is far from Mauthausen she asked for papers to return to Warsaw. Back home she sold the Italian silk and told the engineer that she was giving up on the idea of building barracks, bridges, and roads, but wanted another travel pass to Vienna. He wanted fifteen kilos of tobacco, whole-leaf only.)

Wonderful News

The news about Vienna reaches her friends.

Janka Tempelhof asks Izolda to take her along. Roman the waiter from the Rose asks Izolda to take the Count.

She can't refuse Halina's school friend Janka Tempelhof. And she especially can't turn down the waiter. He tells her that the Count came to Poland to acquire new papers but now he has to go back. He's worth taking along. And what's more, Marynia, the waiter adds, lowering his voice, the man pulls a lot of weight there in Vienna.

She ought to know what Roman means by "new papers." The old ones clearly fell into the wrong hands.

She doesn't hear what's clear, but she definitely understands "he pulls a lot of weight there in Vienna." That's what she's been waiting for! The engineer from Todt issues her a permit—for three people—and she fills the black suitcase with twenty kilos of tobacco.

A few days later the Count has some news. He's been assured (and the source is by all means reliable) that her husband is alive.

A week later he says: I'll try to get him out . . .

She meets the Count in Café Prückel, not far from the Todt office.

She admires his immaculate manners.

She listens to his assurances that her husband is alive.

Wonderful news.

The Scale

Inside Café Prückel she waits for the engineer's Viennese colleague and her next travel permit. Opposite the entrance is a potted ficus and next to that is a mirror. Izolda sits facing the door and watches the street. If she hadn't been facing the door she would have spotted them in the mirror—two men coming into the café, searching for someone . . . They would have seen her back, would have had to walk around the table, look her in the face . . . She still wouldn't have escaped, only gained a minute or two . . . (And what would those minutes have gained her?)

The men step up to her table.

The shorter man asks: Are you waiting for our colleague from Todt?

She nods.

He's waiting for you somewhere else . . .

The men loom over her. The taller one signals for the waiter, she pays, and they leave the café.

They walk past the plane trees and maples of the Ringstrasse, toward the Danube Canal. As soon as they reach the bridge the men grab her by the arms—both at once, without a word, from each side. As if they were afraid she'd jump into the water. She has no intention of jumping. They turn onto Franz-Josefs-Kai and head toward the building she's heard so much about. The building that once was the elegant Hotel Metropol and now houses the Viennese Gestapo.

On the second floor, in room 121, they take her handbag and write down her name. That's all for today. A fat, pinkish officer wearing short Tyrolean trousers and a leather jacket walks her to the prison. Around the corner there is an old man with a weighing machine that he's set up on the pavement along with a little ceramic coin bank. She goes to the old man, removes her shoes, and stands on the scales. For a moment the Gestapo officer loses sight of her. Hey, where are you? he shouts, and sticks his right hand inside his jacket pocket. Don't worry, it's nothing, she assures him, I'm just weighing myself—and slides the balance closer to the middle. Seventy kilograms exactly. Without shoes. She steps off the scales, slips on her shoes, and carefully moves the weight to zero. She remembers that she doesn't have her handbag. She turns to the Gestapo man: Would you mind? He reaches into his left pocket and drops a coin in the bank. It's on the house, he says, and snorts with laughter. Then he turns serious. Why are you doing that? he asks. She shrugs her shoulders, because she really can't say.

In the prison they take away her medallion and hand her a copy of the *Völkischer Beobachter*. As a political prisoner, they explain, she's entitled to a daily newspaper.

Curls

The cell has two bunks, two chairs, and a toilet bowl, all fastened to the wall and the floor. The window is barred and boarded from the outside. Light seeps in through the crack between the plywood and the window frame. The bed folds up like a bunk in a sleeping compartment, except it has a lock—and the key is with the guard. If she sits on the toilet bowl she can rest her legs on one of the chairs. She glances over the newspaper, then folds the printed sheets and tears them into strips, which she wraps around strands of her hair. She sleeps in the curl papers, under a drab-colored, coarse, thin blanket. In the morning they give her a new paper, a cup of ersatz coffee, and a slice of bread. The guard locks the bunk and looks at her curled-up hair. Why are you doing that? he asks. Because . . . She takes out the curl papers and combs her hair. They fall onto her shoulders the way she wanted, with a nice curl at the bottom. Get ready, says the guard, you're going to the Gestapo.

121

The black van with the barred windows stops in the courtyard. Izolda enters room 121. A man is seated behind the desk. He has a nondescript face, light hair, and a darker mustache, closely cropped and stiff. He orders her to stand next to the wall and asks her the purpose of her trip to Vienna. She says that she was carrying tobacco. The Gestapo officer gets up, walks around the desk, slaps her across the face, and returns to his seat. This slap is different from the one in Radom, the motion lasts longer, the hand is heavier, and the pain is more severe. The blow knocks her head against the wall and her false tooth goes flying out. She can feel the sharp metal screw inside her mouth. She looks around anxiously; the tooth is underneath the desk. The

Gestapo man reaches for a cigarette, inhales, looks to see why she is crawling under the desk, examines the tooth, and lets her put it in her pocket. He asks where she got her *Marschbefehl.* She tells him the truth, because the engineer's colleague's signature was on the permit. Why were you going to Vienna? I was carrying tobacco . . . And the Gestapo officer gets up behind the desk.

Regret

Every other day the same van takes her to Gestapo headquarters. The same officer orders her to stand next to the same wall.

On the second day he asks how long she's been working for the Polish underground—*die polnische Untergrundbewegung.* She doesn't know what he's talking about and tells him she isn't working for any underground.

With each blow the back of her head hits the wall. The tooth no longer goes flying out, since she takes it out herself while still in the van. After a few slaps she feels a ringing in her head and has trouble hearing. The Gestapo officer assures her he knows all about the couriers between Poland and Anders's army in Italy. She ran the route from Warsaw to Vienna, but who went from Vienna to Italy? Have you remembered?

Izolda is aghast.

The Count is getting her husband out of the camp.

He's going to need money. She didn't send any packages to Mauthausen and the Gestapo officer thinks she's working for the Polish underground.

The idea of working for the underground didn't even cross her mind. The Polish underground was not her cause. Her cause was her husband and joining the resistance would only jeopardize that. If the underground wanted to help her husband, then maybe she'd do something for them, but since Shayek didn't matter to General Anders, what did she care about him or his couriers?

I don't care about Anders, she repeats, but the Gestapo officer doesn't believe her: You don't fool me, all you Poles are working for the bandits.

She can't contradict him, she has to be like all you Poles. There, you see, the Gestapo officer says, with a note of triumph. So who was the link between Vienna and Italy?

The door to the next room has a thick hook set inside the frame. The Gestapo officer orders her to stand on a stool. He twists her arms behind her back, cuffs them, and hangs her on the hook. First he makes sure it will hold and then he kicks the stool out from under her legs. The pain in her shoulders is excruciating. She dangles just over the floor: if she could only stretch her toes out just a little bit, she thinks, then she could support herself. She tries with all her might to touch the floor.

It's July, the sun is shining, she notices a bright, sunny circle on the floor. She is still conscious. The Gestapo officer paces up and down the room. He's bored, he makes a phone call, arranges to meet someone for a walk on Sunday. He returns to Izolda, adjusts the hook, raising her feet. He tells her he'd prefer to treat a woman more politely, but he has to find out a few details. For example, who ran things to Anders in Italy?

He takes her off the hook and lets her clean up. The room has a marble sink with a crystal mirror—clearly the Metropol was a high-class hotel.

In the mirror she sees a ghastly, swollen face, with eyes popping out of their sockets. She steps back in horror— and so does the face. She steps forward—and the face comes closer. She takes another step and realizes there's nothing to be afraid of because she is walking toward herself.

After the interrogation she returns to the prison, which the locals nicknamed Liesl, from Elisabeth—the street used to be called the Kaiserin-Elisabeth-Prom- enade. Liesl's guards aren't the worst. They unlock her bunk even though it's daytime and give her some cold compresses. A doctor sets her shoulders.

I don't know a thing about any Anders, she tells the guard. Because I'd say something if I did. She is speaking Polish. The guards think she's raving or else revealing some conspiratorial secrets and warn her to calm down. But she's not raving. She would confess any secret—Pol- ish, Jewish, it doesn't matter. First she'd try to make a deal: I'll tell you about Anders, if my husband . . . and maybe she'd get him out of the camp. Unfortunately she doesn't know any secrets. She lies on the bunk and thinks these thoughts with no guilty conscience, only regret.

The Count

Izolda is walking down the corridor to room 121.

And coming from the opposite direction, from the depths of the corridor, is the Count, led by two escorts.

They walk past each other. The Count has a calm, almost cheerful face, he doesn't look at her, doesn't betray her with the slightest gesture. Of course, she thinks—Vienna, Anders, northern Italy . . . it's the Count. He was helping the resistance, not her husband. She feels a bitterness rising within her. The resistance has thousands of people, but she has only one husband, and now he's alone and defenseless, robbed of all help.

That night she dreams about both men. They're inside a church, she's standing off to the side, while the Count leads her husband through all the holy icons, flowers, and candles. She doesn't know if she's allowed to join them, so she stays where she is, and they pass by with indifferent, unseeing faces. Like the Count at the Gestapo headquarters. Like Izolda when she passed her husband's mother

. . . In her dream, her husband is very handsome, slender, his hair like a golden helmet. And his eyes so intensely blue that they can be seen right across the whole church.

On her way to the interrogation, she wonders what her dream might have meant.

She steps into room 121.

The Gestapo officer stands up from behind the desk, steps toward her—and does not put her in handcuffs.

He offers her a chair and says: Please sit down.

She sits.

The Gestapo officer gives a faint smile. We know the truth, he says. You are a Jew, or am I mistaken?

She says nothing.

A Jew. And then? They'll shoot me. Within twenty-four hours, like the Jews at Pawiak. And then? There won't be any stool. There won't be any hook . . .

I think I've had enough, she says in Polish, and hears Halina's voice.

The Gestapo officer doesn't understand Polish.

I'm saying that you are right. I'm Jewish.

Something strange happens. The Gestapo officer's face lights up and he leans toward her with the gallantry of a waiter: Would you like some tea? Coffee? A woman in a summer suit brings in a coffee pot, two cups, and a plate with some cake. The Gestapo officer urges her to eat and starts to explain, in a normal, human voice.

If you were working for General Anders, you would be our enemy. Naturally you would die just like an enemy does. Since you are a Jew, naturally you'll also die, but you aren't guilty . . .

She doesn't quite understand.

You can't be guilty for the faith of your fathers, the Gestapo officer explains.

I can't be guilty, she repeats. But naturally I will die . . .

That's the law, Frau Maria. Good that we got things cleared up . . .

Frau Izolda, she corrects him.

What a beautiful name. But why, *Isolde*, are you admitting that you are a Jew?

Because I've had enough!

That's what her husband's sister Halina had said. Halina, who is no longer alive. Izolda thinks: And I won't worry anymore that I didn't fetch her in time. I won't worry about anyone anymore.

A Walk

Dawn. She lies on her bunk and hears the clanging of keys. The door opens. Two guards are waiting outside her room. She gets up off the bed. They move without haste, she in the middle and the guards on either side. They go down into the yard. It's exercise time and the prisoners are walking one behind the other. She recognizes her husband right away: he's taller than the rest and stands very straight . . . He notices her—and quickly looks the other way. She understands: he's afraid she'll give him away with a look . . . That she'll say something . . . Her husband knows exactly where she is going and wishes she would go a little faster . . . Perhaps he even prays that she will step more quickly . . . There, says the guard, and points to the prison entrance. The gate is open and she can make out a faint light, as though a lantern were burning in the distance. There, the guard repeats. Can you make it by yourself?

She is awakened by the clanging of keys. She jumps up from the bunk, the guard opens the door. No, he hasn't come for her at all. He's simply brought another prisoner.

Nicole

The woman introduces herself: Nicole, I'm French, and you?

Izolda, I'm Jewish . . .

She hasn't said that since the war began. It's not so hard to say, either, perhaps because she says the word in German: *Jüdin.* She tries it out in French: *Juive.* Then a little louder, in three languages: *żydówka, Jüdin, Juive.* It sounds worst in Polish, because of the hard consonants.

Nicole studied history at the Sorbonne, then worked in a factory. She traveled to Vienna with her fiancé. Both were arrested, her fiancé is also locked up in Liesl.

Why did you work in a factory? asks Izolda.

What do you mean why? To be with the proletariat.

And why did you go to Vienna?

What do you mean why? Somebody has to do the work here.

She's never heard that kind of talk before. She figures it must be communist jargon, but she's never seen a communist in person before. Nicole amazes her. Do you think they might kill your fiancé? she asks. *Naturellement.* And then what will happen? Nothing, others will take over his work. I'm asking about you, not about his work. Nothing, either they will kill me as well or else I will try to do the work without him.

She tells Nicole about the Gestapo officer who knew she wasn't guilty.

If I survive this war . . . she says. If my husband survives . . . And if our children are bound to die . . . But what am I blabbing about? she says, and superstitiously spits on the floor of the cell.

Every morning they hear the men marching past their cell on their way to the toilets. Every morning someone whistles a French song outside their door. That's him! Nicole cries out, and rushes to the spyhole, overjoyed. The footsteps fade away and Nicole sings the whole song out loud, all the way to the end.

Following Nicole's example, Izolda sings sentimental hits from before the war: *So what does our love really matter, it's between you and me, who cares if our lives become sadder, that's between you and me, who'll cry after harsh words are spoken . . .*

When she comes to the line *and who'll die when two hearts get broken*, she starts to cry. She pulls her cards out from under the straw mattress and lays them out to read. She just wants to know one thing: What's happening with the king of hearts? Is he once again out the door and on the move?

She made the cards out of the margins of the *Völkischer Beobachter*. She borrowed a safety pin from a guard and marked the spades and clubs by punching different-sized holes in the paper. For the diamonds and hearts she pricked her finger and used her blood. She shuffles carefully, but—unfortunately—the king usually winds up stuck in the middle of the other cards. The only one out the door is herself, the queen of hearts, which Nicole interprets rationally: The Red Army is on its way. Our Soviet brothers are coming closer, they're already in Hungary. Their tanks will attack Vienna at any moment.

Nicole firmly believes that the cell doors will burst open and our Soviet brothers will be standing there and say: Comrades, you are free. (Nicole doesn't know what this will sound like in Russian, so Izolda tells her: *Tovarishchi, vy svobodny.*)

The door does open and the guard—the same one who gave her the safety pin and sometimes brings her an extra portion of bread—says to Izolda: Pack your things, you'll be leaving today. How should I know where?

She says goodbye to Nicole: Greet your Soviet brothers for me (*Bon voyage*, queen of hearts, replies Nicole)— and follows the guard.

The cells in Liesl don't open onto corridors but are arranged around a kind of hall with a stairwell in the middle. Izolda goes down the stairs to the office, where they return her medallion and her café-au-lait handbag from Herse's. It has a comb and a Bakelite compact (she left the silver one with Stefa). She adds her curling paper and the cards she made from the newspaper. She also puts in her false tooth, although that doesn't make much sense: the Gestapo officer knocked out two more, in the front. She didn't pick them up, she didn't have the strength, but she carefully stows the artificial one, even though it's no longer of use. The guard waits for her to pack her belongings and takes her to the black van.

Travel

She's traveling on board a regular train, third class. There are eight people in her compartment, including Janka Tempelhof. Their bags are stowed on the shelves overhead. It's a warm September day and the Viennese Jews are dressed lightly. They've packed their furs and sweaters in their suitcases, since they might have to stay there a little longer. "There" is the word they use to mean the place where they will live and work. She explains that "there" means a camp, possibly Auschwitz. They don't know that word and don't try to repeat it, the Polish name is too difficult. The Viennese Jews ask how she knows it's a camp and that no one comes back from there. Everybody knows that. In Poland every child knows that. In Poland . . . the Viennese Jews say with disdain. Maybe no one comes back in Poland, but we're from Vienna, not Poland, we are going to work.

Night falls. What are you thinking about? Janka Tempelhof whispers. About my husband, my mother in Warsaw . . . Izolda had read a brief notice on the third page of the *Völkischer Beobachter* about an uprising in Warsaw. Can you send packages to Mauthausen during an uprising?

Both of Janka's parents died in the ghetto in Łódź. She doesn't have any friends . . .

What do you mean you don't have any friends? Izolda is surprised.

They thought I was showing off, because I always know better, Janka confesses. They were wrong, I wasn't showing off . . .

Maybe you really did know better, she consoles Janka. I, for example, knew worse.

And what of it? Janka whispers. Now we're both on transport number 47. Together . . .

She's surprised that Janka knows the number of their transport. How do you know that?

I just do . . . Janka smiles in the dark. Like I said, I always know better . . .

They pass a lit sign: Ostrava. The train slows down. Izolda stops listening to Janka Tempelhof's confessions and stands up. Will you jump with me? she asks. Janka doesn't answer. Izolda grabs the canvas sash used to lower the window, climbs on the seat and sticks one leg out of the open window. An older man by the window grabs her other leg. He is surprisingly strong, they scuffle and someone cries out: Don't be stupid, we're going to work, you'll get us all in trouble! Janka just sits there and does nothing. The gendarmes come running down the corridor, she quickly raises the window and returns to her seat. What's going on? One gendarme examines the compartment. Nothing's going on, says the Viennese Jew who pulled her from the window. Everyone's very comfortable.

It gets light.

The sun rises.

The train slows down again. They read the sign on the station: Dziedzice. She senses that the train is turning onto a branch line.

Look, she says. Look how bright blue and clean the sky is in Poland.

A Bucket of Water

The passengers from the Viennese train assemble in front of a barracks. They are a little uneasy: their suitcases are lying on the ground, in a huge pile. Won't they be damaged? Or lost? And where do they get them back? Izolda isn't worried. Her bag is on the pile, but for the moment she doesn't need the curling papers, the cards, or the artificial tooth.

An SS man gives a signal and two prisoners approach the group, each carrying a dirty striped cap: the passengers are told to toss in their money and jewelry. She tosses in her Mother of God medallion, the gift from Lilusia. Someone asks when to expect a receipt for their valuables. The prisoners don't say anything. Someone else repeats the question a little louder. The Viennese Jews anxiously study the two prisoners—their silence, their empty, indifferent eyes. Izolda watches them as well. Their eyes aren't out of their sockets and their shoulder blades haven't been dislocated. They're wearing striped suits—but so? What's so terrible about stripes?

The SS man orders everyone to undress.

Then he orders them to approach—one at a time, calmly. He looks each one over and either waves his hand or nods his head. He does this fleetingly, carelessly, as if he didn't want to. His hand gesture is also careless and sloppy.

She steps up to the SS man. She has smooth skin and a small red spot next to her breast. The German stops her and stares at the spot—a long time, several seconds—then raises his hand, meaning she should stand to the right. After Izolda comes Janka Tempelhof. She has a very nice figure, not tall, and a kind, calm smile. The SS man sends her to the right as well.

Two groups form, right and left. The groups keep growing, the one on the left more quickly than the one on the right. The old man who pulled her from the window approaches the SS man, bashfully covering his underbelly. He looks shorter and thinner than he did wearing clothes, his shoulder is crooked and juts out to the left. The Viennese woman next to Izolda asks if she thinks the older people will get easier work, because her father was sent to the left. Izolda reassures her: I'm sure they will, you shouldn't be worried. The woman's father knows several languages, maybe they'll assign him to an office . . . the woman consoles herself. I'm sure of it, Izolda says to encourage her. My father also knew a lot of languages, she adds, imagining her father standing naked, defenseless, and embarrassed among the specialists that knew German.

A man from the group on the left takes a few steps toward the SS man, smiles politely, and says: Sir, we are thirsty, could we please ask for some water?

The SS man smiles back. The gentleman is thirsty, he says to the prisoners who collected the jewelry. They took it away and have now returned wearing their caps. Bring the gentleman a little water . . . The prisoners leave again and return with a bucket full of water. They place it on the ground. The polite Viennese Jew looks for a cup. You'll have to drink from the bucket, the SS man says, and signals to the prisoners. They grab the man under the arm, bend his neck, and shove his head into the water. The man squirms for air, kicking and pushing with his legs . . . Eventually he calms down. His body sags. The prisoners let go, step back, and stand off to the side. The man's body slides to the ground. Is anyone else thirsty? asks the SS man.

A Number

They give her clothing: a rough cretonne dress with a
flower print, a black sweater, a number—preceded by the
letter *A* and tattooed on her forearm—and a place to
sleep. The barracks have three rows of bunks, with three
levels to a row. Izolda's place is on the top. The bunk
could fit four women lying on their back. But it has to
accommodate nine, so in the evening they all lie on their
left side, facing the wall. Their knees are bent and their
bottoms press against the stomachs of the women behind
them, while someone else's buttocks press against their
own. During the night they shift positions, all at once,
onto their right side.

After two days Izolda and Janka discover that they
were given the wrong numbers. The inmate functionary
in charge of the tattooing etches a horizontal line through
the old numbers and gives them new ones, this time with
a small triangle. You're lucky, the woman tells them. That
triangle is Jewish all right, but those numbers mean you
came here with a record.

They have a record because they were in prison.

They're lucky because people with a prison record
aren't subject to the selection.

There had been a mistake when they arrived. Transports were coming in from the Łódź ghetto and in the
confusion their group was treated like the Jews from
Łódź. The selection was illegal. Unlike what happened

to the other Jews. Those Jews were in a normal transport, they didn't have prison records, and their selection was in order.

For some time she's been staring at the sweater worn by one of the inmates working in the office. The sweater is knitted from colorful bits of yarn. Izolda moves closer. She can see a few knots and a dark pink lining sticking out from the bottom and at the sleeves. It's the same sweater her friend Basia Gajer, née Maliniak, wore when she left for Honduras.

They go back to their barracks. On the way she tells Janka about Basia, Honduras, and the sweater. Could it be a sign? she wonders.

That's very possible, says Janka, but who knows what it means.

It was at Basia's where I met my husband. I went in for a minute just to thread my shoelaces and he was standing by the stove warming his hands on the tiles. Like this . . . and then he let them drop, they looked so helpless somehow . . .

Your friend Basia is telling you something, Janka Tempelhof states. Maybe you'll survive Auschwitz?

The Deal

It's still dark and they're standing in front of the barracks. The *Stubendienst* and the *Aufseherin* take the roll call and report to the SS men. The numbers don't match up, they keep counting and counting, the roll call drags on for hours.

During roll call the sky has two colors—deep gray on the darker side and a reddish violet on the lighter side. Clouds pass under the light, filling themselves with gold and violet, and float down toward the earth. She'd never seen the sun rise more beautifully than it did at Auschwitz.

She stands next to two women from Silesia. The older one reminds her of her mother, especially her eyes, her mouth, and her cheeks.

She makes a deal with God. I will help this woman, she says, and in exchange you will help my mother . . . Agreed?

She shields the woman from the wind. Other prisoners vie for the place in the middle, where it's warmer—Izolda immediately stands on the outside, to shelter the woman who looks like her mother.

The woman smiles in gratitude, folds her hands, and whispers something.

Izolda leans in toward the woman . . .

Please don't disturb me at the moment, the woman says, I'm praying.

The woman is also talking with God. Do you see? I'm helping her. Don't forget: We have a deal.

Presents

They send their shoes and clothing to be disinfected. The lice are killed, but not the nits, and new lice emerge after a few days. As a result of the disinfection she loses her only photo of her husband. She was carrying it in her shoe and didn't manage to save it in time. The picture showed a young man on skis wearing a Norwegian sweater, with ski poles in both hands and a snowy mountain slope in the distance.

They've been placed in quarantine. They aren't sent to work: after roll call they sit on their bunks.

In the afternoon they're given soup made from rutabaga or potato peelings. She prefers rutabaga since it doesn't have sand. In the evening they receive half a boiled potato and some bread. They eat the potato and save the bread for breakfast; the morning hunger is harder to bear. They sleep on their bread so no one steals it during the night.

The soup is brought in wooden barrels with handles through which a wooden pole is inserted. The two functionaries who bring the soup call the barrels *faski*. They pour the soup into the bowls, take the *faski* out, and set them next to the barracks wall. In the afternoon there is another short roll call. The women dash out and fall on the barrels, chasing away the swarms of enormous, sluggish horseflies and scraping the rest of the soup off the bottom with their bare hands. They spend nearly twenty minutes between the barracks. During this time Izolda looks for women from the uprising in Warsaw and asks about Pańska Street. Pańska doesn't exist, says a woman from the uprising. What about number 6 Mariańska Street? Mariańska isn't there either, don't you realize that Warsaw doesn't exist anymore? She's frightened at the idea that Warsaw might not be there. Because then maybe Lilusia isn't there, or Terenia, or Mrs. Krusiewicz. So who will send packages to Mauthausen?

Sonia Landau runs up—she works in an office and is allowed to move about the camp. She brings presents: a small onion, a towel, and warm stockings. Used, but good quality, she says proudly, from the Hungarian Jews. Izolda asks her about the Hungarian Jews, because they aren't in quarantine. Sonia points at the smokestack by the crematorium and says: That's where they are now.

In the evening Izolda puts on the stockings and folds the towel under her head. It must have been packed between clothes inside a suitcase. This Hungarian Jew had some nice perfume, she thinks as she falls asleep.

During the night she gives the onion to the *Stubendienst* and is allowed to go to the toilet. As she crouches over the bucket next to the wall of the barracks, she smells an odor of burned goose feathers. A thick, dark brown column of smoke is rising from the crematorium and is quickly swallowed by the sky.

Talent

A package arrives for the woman who looks like Izolda's mother. Delighted, she sits on the top bunk across from Izolda, takes the parcel out of the box, removes the paper, looks at it tenderly, and puts it back. She raises her head and signals for Izolda to join her. Izolda hurries over and stands on the middle bunk, so that her face is level with the package and the other woman's hands. She wants to give me something, Izolda thinks gratefully—maybe a clove of garlic or even a heel of bread . . .

The woman takes out a white silk slip. She brushes it off, smooths it out, and says: It's nice, isn't it? This can be traded for food. Take care of it, would you, Izolda? Sorry for the trouble but you're more talented at that sort of thing than we are.

Izolda is still standing on the bunk. Still smiling . . . The woman's friend looks at her uneasily: Is something wrong, Izolda?

She trades the slip for a single, fairly large unpeeled potato and continues to protect the woman from the wind. Thanks to her talents, she's made a deal with God and has to fulfill her side of the bargain.

Standing at roll call, she promises herself that she'll never have any more Jewish talents or Jewish anything. Assuming, of course, that she survives the war. And her husband won't either. Or their children. And their

children will not die guiltless of everything but the faith
of their fathers . . .

The woman who looks like her mother leans over and
says: Are you saying something, Izolda?

She shakes her head: Please don't disturb me at the
moment, I'm praying.

The Exam

The Germans are moving the prisoners from Auschwitz.
No one knows where to: some say deep inside the Reich
and others say to be gunned down. Nurses are sent with
every transport, so maybe it's not to be gunned down.
Dr. Mengele is standing on the platform, looking over
the people being shipped away. Some consider this a bad
sign, others think the opposite.

She tells Janka Tempelhof that she's going to volunteer
for a transport (the trains are moving west, aren't they,
perhaps in the direction of Mauthausen?).

On the platform they both leave the crowd of people
waiting and approach Dr. Mengele.

Izolda explains that they are nurses. With hospital
experience. (It's true: Janka took courses at the Maltese
Hospital. Her theoretical knowledge was very good but
she was clumsy and ended up working in the office.)
Could Herr Doktor allow them to join the transport?

"Herr Doktor" is handsome, well groomed, carefully shaven, and perfectly clean. He looks both women over.

Do you remember . . . (he thinks for a moment). Naturally you remember how arterial bleeding differs from venous bleeding . . .

In Polish she would answer without hesitation that arterial blood is oxygenated, consequently it is bright red in color and spurts from the wound. Venous blood, on the other hand . . . but she doesn't know the German words. She says a little incoherently: *Das Blut, im Blut ist Sauerstoff* . . . Fortunately Janka answers fluently and in complete sentences. Dr. Mengele nods his head exactly like Dr. Munwes at the hospital on Czysta Street, when he asked Izolda to describe the symptoms of typhus. Like any doctor would, hearing a young nurse give the correct answer, especially a good-looking young nurse, despite a few missing teeth.

How many times does a heart beat per minute?

This question is only meant for her. He sounds easygoing, like a professor who doesn't want his students to fail their exam.

That depends, she answers.

Oh? On what?

On whether a person is afraid or not. And on how afraid they are.

The examiner bursts into a loud, friendly laugh that shows the gap between his two front teeth. Diastema . . .

she remembers reading about it in her nursing course-book. That kind of gap is called a diastema.

The *Aufseherin* standing behind Mengele writes down their numbers. A couple of days later during roll call they are called out and told to report to the next transport.

Daemon

She has her own bunk, two whole blankets, the roll call lasts half an hour, the soup is free of sand, and their guards are not SS but Wehrmacht—men too old for the front and war invalids. In other words, Guben is wonderful.

They work in a factory on the other side of the river. They sit in front of an assembly belt, each prisoner stationed between two German workers. The objects on the belt need something screwed on or soldered, the German workers make sure things are done properly.

But there are three things wrong with the camp in Guben.

The first is the sleepless nights, because of the women screaming for bread. The bread is brought in the evening, the *Stubendienst* is supposed to cut each loaf into five even pieces. The women crowd around, watchful and wary. The knife is dull, the bread is made with sawdust and crumbles easily, the crowd makes sure everything is fair. They weigh each portion (having constructed a scale from two boxes and a piece of string) and loudly count the crumbs. The tension rises and falls. When the knife plunges into the dough the women concentrate in silence and then scream out loud if one portion is smaller than the others. Janka Tempelhof tries to calculate how many calories are in the crumbs and how many are spent in the screaming. She determines that more are lost in the screaming, but no one wants to listen to her.

The second thing wrong is the distance from Mauthausen. The front is getting closer and closer and soon she'll be cut off from her husband for good.

The third thing wrong is the name Regensberg. She can't travel across all of Germany and Austria with a Jewish name . . .

Do you have a plan, Janka Tempelhof interrupts, or are you counting on a twist of fate?

She has a plan. First she'll return to Cottbus; it isn't far, just two or three stations away.

She'll find the nice clerk (who wished her good luck).

She'll say she was on a transport from the Warsaw Uprising, but didn't know where they were headed so she broke off.

She'll apologize for escaping from her assigned labor.

She'll go back to the canvas mill and figure things out from there.

Look . . . Janka Tempelhof explains. Here you have your own bunk. You have two blankets and no sand in the soup. Things are good, why go to Cottbus?

So I can be Maria Pawlicka, she explains all over again. Forever. No more Izolda Regensberg.

Janka thinks a moment and says: That's your daemon

again sending you on your way, so you better go. You should listen to what your daemon is telling you.

(Frankly she doesn't have any idea what a daemon is, but she's too embarrassed to ask. She guesses that it's someone that even Janka Tempelhof doesn't dare argue with.)

Armchair. Credit

. . . If they hadn't taken her for a prostitute, she wouldn't have stopped in on Mateusz the caretaker,

she wouldn't have learned about Mauthausen,

she wouldn't have traveled to Vienna.

If she hadn't gone to Vienna, she would have stayed in Warsaw. She would have died in the uprising, in the basement, together with her mother.

If she hadn't escaped from Guben, they would have sent her on with the other women.

She would have landed at Bergen-Belsen,

in the middle of a typhus epidemic.

She would have died of typhus together with Janka Tempelhof.

Evidently God had decided she was meant to survive the war.

Or not. He had decided that she was meant to die and she opposed His verdict with all her strength. That's the only reason she survived. And no God can claim credit. It was her doing and hers alone.

Happiness

She forgoes her daily portion of bread and after five days the *Stubendienst* gives her a whole loaf. She trades the bread for ten marks and a set of dentures. The dentures have a fairly sizable gold bridge and part of a gold tooth. It seems they belonged to a woman.

The factory is some way off and on cold days the women are allowed to take blankets. They wrap them around their heads and before entering the hall they leave them in the cloakroom.

She walks to the factory. She leaves her blanket. She takes a German worker's coat off the hook and carries it to the other side of the cloakroom. She feels a little bad, but she can't make her escape wrapped up in a blanket from the camp.

They're done for the day, and go to the cloakroom ahead of the German workers.

She folds up the stolen coat and covers it with her blanket. Then she joins the column of women prisoners leaving the factory.

It's getting dark and there is fog.

The column crosses the Neisse River and turns to the left, toward the yellow light of the lanterns. Izolda turns to the right . . . She drops her blanket and quickly passes several streets.

She senses that she's being followed. She turns around and sees a bicycle and a faint blur of light: the bicyclist is carrying a lantern. The camp guards are equipped with bicycles and lanterns—evidently they're already looking for her.

She pushes open a gate, hears the crunch of gravel underfoot, and crouches against a fence. She is in a garden and looming behind her is what appears to be a single-story house.

The bicycle comes creaking down the street. It stops at the gate. She hears steps . . . a man has climbed off, he's walking down the gravel path. She clings to the fence. The man, barely visible in the darkness, passes her and opens the door. Now she has a clear view of him: he has a rifle slung over his shoulder. He doesn't go in. He must be listening, waiting for some sound, perhaps the sound of her breathing. She waits as well. She hears her heart pounding, just like in the ghetto when she was standing next to the door with the padlock. The gendarme probably hears her heart as well. She can't bear it any longer and tears away from the fence. I'm coming, she says, under her breath. The gendarme is silent. She takes a step in his direction and says louder: Please don't shoot, I'm coming . . .

She walks up to the house.

Here I am, she says, to the entrance, but no one answers.

She's at the doorstep. There isn't any gendarme. There isn't anyone at all. That's strange, she thinks. I'm probably hallucinating. Out of fear? I'm not scared, but I'm having hallucinations. For the first time. Though I'm really not afraid . . .

She leans against the door. She tears a strip from the coat lining and wraps it around her head like a turban, to cover her black roots. The lining keeps sliding down over her eyes, evidently her hands are shaking. That's strange, she thinks. I'm not afraid and yet my hands are shaking.

She approaches the station from the back, crossing the rails. A train has stopped on the tracks and she hears banging: a tapper is checking the wheels. She hides behind a freight car, and after the tapper passes she climbs onto the raised platform at the back. Inside is a bench and a small, rectangular window. She stands by the window. The train starts to roll. It passes the tangle of tracks and moves out across the fields, through lashing wind and rain. She stands next to the window and feels a wave of happiness.

She doesn't know where the train is headed.

She doesn't have any documents.

She doesn't have anything but a German worker's overcoat, a Hungarian Jew's stockings, and a section of Jewish dentures with a gold tooth.

She's riding a night train through Germany and feels such joy that she starts to cry.

I'm free, she says out loud.

And I'm alive.

And he's alive.

And I am free.

And everything will be good . . .

She picks up the coat and wipes her nose on a piece of lining.

Armchair. Foreign Languages

She will try (in spite of everything) to tell her story: dae-mon—escape—freight car—and to explain how happy she was at that moment, and how happiness can suddenly overcome a person in absurd situations.

Her daughter will translate into Hebrew, her grand-daughter will nod understandingly: Happiness can sur-prise you, that's true . . . And what happened next?

Next came a train station and the train stopped. A conductor came in, astonished at what he saw. *Was machen Sie hier?* he shouted. She answered very calmly: "Nothing really, I'm headed to Cottbus." (In dangerous situations, she lectures her granddaughter, it's always good to . . . how can I explain it . . . it's good to maintain a certain air of superiority.) Cottbus?—the conductor was even more amazed. We're headed in the opposite direction! To which she replied, still calmly: Really? In that case I must have got on the wrong train.

Her granddaughter will worry: The conductor could have called the gendarmes or even the SS.

No, he didn't call anyone. He was a harmless man in

late middle age and she always had a way with older men.

Her daughter and granddaughter will smile and for a moment they'll talk about her good looks. Her daughter will say that she was beautiful, just like Elizabeth Taylor, and her granddaughter will state that she's still very beautiful, and then what?

She jumped out of the car and changed trains. She made her way to Cottbus. She found the clerk with the notebook and apologized for running away.

(What's the Hebrew word for war? she asks all of a sudden. *Milchama*. Clerk? *Pakid*. Notebook? *Machberet* . . . Such bizarre words, how can anyone learn such a language? They're extraordinary words, her daughter will say. Listen: *machberet* . . . You think desert and sand and cliffs, and it's nothing more than a notebook.)

The clerk asked where she was coming from. Izolda told her she'd been on one of the transports out of Warsaw after the uprising. They were headed in this direction but she wasn't sure where to and feared it might be to a camp, so she broke away . . .

Her daughter will interrupt, telling her to explain about the Warsaw Uprising. Of course her granddaughter had learned about it in school, but it's easy to get all the uprisings mixed up . . .

Unfortunately, the nice clerk was only in charge of farmworkers, but Izolda had been assigned to the canvas mill and someone else was in charge of the factories. And that person was eating supper.

Why so many details, her daughter will grow impatient. What difference does it make which clerk and what they ate?

It makes all the difference in the world! The nice clerk remembered that my name was Pawlicka, don't you understand? Maria Pawlicka and not Regensberg! She remembered, but she couldn't help me, and the person who could help me was eating supper, she'd finished work and had gone home!

What are you arguing about? her granddaughter will ask.

Her daughter will explain the difference between the clerks, and her granddaughter will start to look at her watch.

They sent me to their superior . . .

Wir beide sollen das Gesetz achten, hab' ich nicht Recht? he said. Which means: We both ought to respect the law, isn't that right? And the law, my dear, stipulates that people who desert their place of work are sent to the penal camp.

Schwetig an der Oder

In the morning they braid straw (shoe coverings for use on the front).

After that they pump water. The water spills, their toes freeze to the ground because their shoes are full of holes, the iron pump handle burns their hands. I can't take it anymore, she cries out, and Irma, who is carrying full buckets to the cistern, has the presence of mind to ask her what she plans to do instead. Are you going to run away again? Stop grousing and pump, there's nothing a person can't take.

Irma has a degree in forestry. She escaped from a sub-camp of Ravensbrück, they captured her as she was washing her legs in a stream. They didn't let her put on her shoes and brought her barefoot to Schwetig. Every day she wraps her feet in rags and straw.

They sleep on the ground, on straw mattresses. Irma lies next to her and tells stories about trees and how clever they are.

Do you know that maple seeds spin in different ways? Half of them spin to the right and half to the left, so that the wind carries the seeds in all directions. (Izolda wants to make Irma feel good and is suitably amazed.)

Do you know why sequoia bark doesn't burn? That's how the tree protects itself in case of forest fire. (Really? That's amazing.)

And do you know why aspen leaves quake? It's not because they're afraid . . .

After pumping water they're told to form two concentric circles and forced to run. A female guard uses a whip on the women in the smaller circle. For the big circle another guard goads the runners with a dog. The prisoners can choose between the whip and the dog.

After running comes exercise with *Aufseherin* Piontek.

Alles raus! she shouts, and the women have to run out of the barracks. *Alles rein!* and they have to run back. *Alles raus!*—they run out. *Alles rein!*—they run back.

Piontek loves her work, she doesn't go home until dark.

At morning roll call they read out over a dozen names, including Maria Pawlicka (Auschwitz, adds the *Aufseherin*) and Irma Jabłońska (Ravensbrück).

Izolda tells Irma what they do at Auschwitz with captured escapees. They hang a plank around their neck saying: *Hurra hurra ich bin wieder da*—Hooray hooray I'm back today. And then they are marched to the gallows.

Irma consoles her: You escaped from Guben, not Auschwitz, but they both know she could easily be eligible for the plank.

Izolda tears the fur collar off her German coat.

She trades it for a pair of shoes.

Very decent leather lace-up shoes—which she gives to Irma Jabłońska.

You see that, don't you? she asks God. I'm helping her. And in return, you . . . She hesitates. You do what you think is right.

She says goodbye to Irma.

A gendarme takes her to the train along with a group of prisoners.

The train moves out.

The train stops.

Hours pass, the train doesn't move.

The train reverses direction.

The train gains speed.

Now there's no question about it: the train really is heading back, it really is.

Is it possible that God liberated Auschwitz especially for her? In return for the shoes she gave Irma Jabłońska?

That's impossible. That's just absurd. But the train was turned back and Auschwitz was free.

The March Out

The last prisoners are given bread, coarse undergarments, and heavy canvas clothing.

Prisoners, guards, *Aufseherinnen*, and dogs line up five abreast and march west toward Berlin.

A stream of German refugees move down the middle of the road, on bicycles or horse carts or else on foot, loaded down with rucksacks, suitcases, bundles, carpets, blankets, bedsheets . . . No one is guarding them with dogs and no one is shooting at them and no one does them any harm.

Do you know anyone in Berlin? asks a girl marching next to her. I can give you an address, but how about you? You don't even have a collar on your coat.

But I do have this . . . Izolda reaches for the dentures with the gold bridge that she's kept hidden in her under-wear. She breaks off the tooth. The girl looks at it, puts it in her pants and whispers: Eichenallee, the last house

on the corner. Head toward the Olympic Stadium . . .
Say hello from Edyta Baka. Mention the kayaks at Lut-
tensee . . .

They sleep in empty stables by the side of the road.
Izolda gets up before dawn and listens. Nothing is happening, the dogs are quiet (they're either asleep or have
simply decided there's no use guarding anymore). She
goes onto the road and mixes with the stream of refugees.

Maria Hunkert

Izolda gives Edyta's friend the rest of the gold dental
bridge in exchange for a little money, a dress that's too
short but warm, and a ball of string. She ties the string
around her waist and thighs and fashions a perfectly ser-
viceable garter belt. The dress doesn't cover it completely,
but her coat does. The friend's husband repairs her shoes
and now she's ready for the road.

She goes to the Görlitzer Bahnhof. At the counter
they ask for her travel permit, she can obtain one at the
National Socialist League of German Women.

She tells the German Women that she's an ethnic German from Poland, that she was escaping on foot with the
refugees, that she lost her bag in an air raid, and that her
name is Maria Hunkert. The German Women believe her
and she's authorized to buy a ticket all the way to Vienna.

She has to change trains in Dresden: she arrives in the

evening, her connection is in the morning. Boys from the Hitler Youth are standing by to assist the refugees, carrying their belongings, and helping them onto trucks. One of the boys asks her why she doesn't have any bags. That's a long story, she says, and sighs. I understand, whispers the boy from the Hitler Youth. You went through hell, didn't you, ma'am?—and squeezes her hand in sympathy. Beds for the refugees have been set up in schoolrooms. She is given coffee, bread, and a clean towel, and goes to bed. In the morning they issue her sandwiches for the road ("food rations") and cigarettes ("care rations"). The trucks take everyone to the station, and the serious, concerned boys from the Hitler Youth escort them to the trains.

In a cheap Viennese hotel she trades her cigarettes ("care rations") for a room for three days, as well as some food coupons. She buys a newspaper. She scans the ads for two notices: a dental technician and employment for a young, energetic woman, to begin immediately.

Zimmermann

The restaurant belongs to a Herr Zimmermann (which is made clear by a sign spanning the entire room: "Herr Zimmermann reminds his guests that the table settings are his property only"). Izolda sits down at a table. A waiter takes her order: two bowls of soup, two portions of meat, two desserts . . . The waiter cuts the coupons from her ration card and asks how she would like to be served. Everything at once, she says. Everything? You must be very hungry, he smiles. She ought to smile back but she can't, since she's still missing her front teeth. She's lucky her mouth is shaped the way it is: her lips conceal her upper teeth completely—at least as long as she doesn't smile.

The waiter comes back and covers the entire table with the dishes she ordered. What about cutlery? she calls out. You forgot the cutlery! I didn't forget, the waiter says, but you didn't take off your coat. Please take your coat to the cloakroom, give me your ticket, and I'll bring you some cutlery. Do you realize how many foreigners are running around Vienna these days? Frenchmen, Italians, Poles, Yugoslavs—and they're all trying to steal something. But it's not such a huge concern, is it, *gnädige Frau*? All you have to do is take your coat to the cloakroom.

She can't take off her coat because then everyone would see her improvised garter belt.

She can't eat with her hands, because she would draw attention to herself.

She is on the verge of tears.

A man at the table next to hers stands up. He calls the waiter over and says something. The waiter takes the man's dirty cutlery and brings it back washed, in a starched white napkin. The man lays the cutlery on the table in front of Izolda, bows, and says that there is a very nice café nearby. If she would care to join him for some coffee after her meal . . .

She tries not to eat ravenously.

She tries to cut with the knife and pick up with the fork.

She tries to remember to hold the knife in her right hand and the fork in her left . . .

The man takes the cutlery after she's done and waits for his cloakroom ticket. She gets up and hurries out of Herr Zimmermann's restaurant. She fishes the piece of newspaper out of her pocket ("young, energetic, to begin immediately") and checks the address.

Kaisertorte

The old lady leans on her walking stick and asks what she can do.

Everything, she says, without hesitation. She can clean, cook, launder, and speak French. And what about baking? Do you know how to bake a *Kaisertorte*?

Unfortunately she doesn't know how to bake a *Kaisertorte* (she doesn't even know what it looks like). However, she quickly adds, she does know how to bake *Buchteln*— yeast rolls filled with preserves.

The lady is genuinely surprised: a person who doesn't know how to bake a torte is looking for work in a Viennese household?

Madame . . . she turns to the lady and then goes silent, unsure of what she really intends to say. *Madame* . . . she repeats and hears herself delivering a tirade about the end of the world. The world is falling apart. The world is being bathed in blood and tears (she hopes she said it correctly in German) and meanwhile you, *madame*, cannot be happy unless you have your torte?!

The lady listens very attentively, without interrupting.

Listen, my dear, she says at last, you have a pretty face. And the lecture you've just given me is very interesting, but you don't know how to bake a *Kaisertorte*—and with that she points her black lacquered stick at the door.

Schwester Maria

At the Employment Office they're seeking doctors and experienced nurses. She assures them that she's an experienced nurse (she lost her diploma in all the fighting) and shows the travel permit issued to the ethnic German Maria Hunkert. She's directed to a military hospital. She puts on a long blue dress, apron, cape, and bonnet. They assign her to the third floor, with eighty wounded men— Wehrmacht and SS.

She washes, massages, changes bedpans, uncovers the wounds before the doctor makes his rounds, and bandages them up afterward. The wounds fill with pus, the bandages stick, she moistens them with hydrogen peroxide, and removes them with great patience and care, one millimeter at a time. The doctor watches her work. I see you haven't grown indifferent, he says. You know why that is? Because you haven't seen death. She doesn't contradict him, doesn't look up from her bandages.

(The doctor is old, he spent both wars in military hospitals, but she feels more mature. Perhaps because she has seen different types of death. The death he knows is fast, from the front lines. In the ghetto and in Auschwitz it was a slow expiring. It's dying, not death, that makes you mature, she thinks as she changes a bandage.)

One of her charges is eighteen years old and has an infected stomach wound. In his fever he calls out, "Mama!"

Another has red hair and freckles and watery, lashless eyes. His leg has been cut off above his knee and his wound won't heal. He never moans, but he occasionally faints when she changes his bandage.

The oldest is forty years old. He has an amputated hand and burned-out eyes. He used to be a stage designer and talks about a production he never managed to finish.

Everything was supposed to be gray and black, he says—everything except for her, and she was going to be in yellow and red ocher.

Who is she? asks Izolda.

Joanna . . . Do you see her? Do you see? In yellow and red ocher. And gold.

She places a gauze wick on his eyes and lifts his amputated arm. Under his armpit, level with his heart, is a tattoo showing his blood type. The distinctive dark blue letters are the same size as her number from Auschwitz.

You're looking at me, the SS man surmises. And what do you see?

She studies his emaciated face and the eyeballs without pupils. Where exactly do yellow and red ocher fall in the spectrum?

Every morning the enemy planes cross into Austrian airspace. She quickly moves the wounded onto stretchers, helps out the orderlies, and everyone clambers down into the shelter. "*Licht, Luft, und Sonne . . .*"—the designer shouts out the German propaganda slogan. Light, air, and sunshine! Sunshine, air, and light! Air and light! Air and light! Air . . . In the afternoon the radio calls off the alarm and they return to the third floor. It's nothing, she calms the patients down, in just a minute you'll be able to relax.

The Red Army enters Vienna.

The hospital puts out white flags and Red Cross signs. The nurses and doctors stand to attention inside their rooms, their aprons spotless white.

The Russians burst in, rifles at the ready. *Kto SS?* Who is SS? they ask the doctor.

The doctor says nothing.

They go to her. *SS?*

She, too, says nothing.

The soldier points the rifle barrel in her direction:

A teper, sestra?—And now, nurse? *Uzhe znayesh*—Now do you know? She unbuttons her cuff and rolls up her sleeve. She shows them the number and says: Auschwitz. I'm Polish. *Uzhe znayesh?*

They call an officer.

She stands there with her rolled-up sleeve. Auschwitz . . . Oświęcim . . . Polish . . .

All the more so, says the officer. Are you saying they didn't kill any of yours?

They killed everyone. *Vsekh ubili.*

So get even . . . The officer claps her on the shoulder. Now you can take revenge. *Nu? Kotory SS?*—Well? Which one is SS?

But I don't know. I know who doesn't have eyes and who doesn't have legs. But who is SS, I don't know— *ya ne znayu.*

The soldiers withdraw.

The designer covers his face with a towel and cries out loud. The doctor leans over her number: *Schwester Maria, mein Gott . . .*

She lets down her sleeve. Takes off her bonnet. Walks down three flights of stairs, one step at a time, holding on to the rail. She feels that all her energy has escaped.

She thinks: What will happen now? I have to go. I have to make it to Mauthausen but I don't have the strength.

She leans against the hospital wall.

The war is over, she thinks. And I am alive.

The war is finished. So why aren't I the least bit happy?

The Bicycle

Nu chto, sestra?——What's the matter, nurse?

She opens her eyes. The officer who told her to get even is standing next to her. You thought we wouldn't find them. But we found them, don't you worry.

And the one without eyes?

Every single one. Feeling sorry?

Not sorry, she shakes her head, just tired. How am I going to get to Mauthausen if I don't have any strength?

Take a bicycle, the officer suggests. You want a bike? Wait, I'll find one for you.

He goes to the hospital yard and comes back with a noisy, rundown piece of junk.

He asks how she knows Russian.

My mother spoke it.

And German?

My father spoke it.

(She thinks: Why am I talking about both of them in the past tense?)

So get on and go——the officer waves goodbye.

Listen . . . she calls after him. *Kuda?* Where should I go now? Do you happen to know?

The officer thinks a moment.

You'll need papers——*bumaga. Bumaga* and headquarters. Go straight, past the roundabout.

A crowd is milling in front of the Soviet headquarters. Czechs, French, Yugoslavs, Poles . . . wearing striped prison issue, civilian rags. Prisoners from the camps and Stalags, forced laborers . . . They come from everywhere—except Mauthausen.

One of the Poles has heard about some abandoned apartments belonging to Gestapo officers and SS men. They're free for the taking but you need permission from the Russians.

She parks her bicycle outside the entrance.

She shows the officer at the desk her number from Auschwitz and *grazhdanka Pavlitskaya* receives her *bumaga*—Citizen Pavlitskaya receives her official papers: "The headquarters of the fourth district hereby grants permission to occupy residence in the Operngasse . . ." She leaves the building.

Next to her beaten-up piece of junk she finds a splendid shiny, chrome-plated bicycle. The guard understands her look. *Beri*, he says, take it—and wheels the bike toward her. *Beri*, he encourages her. *Vsyo ravno, voyna* . . . Who cares, it's war . . .

Father

The apartment on Operngasse has everything: clothing, dishes, bedding. She finds a down cover, folds out the sofa bed, and falls asleep.

She wakes in the dark and doesn't know where she is. Strange. Throughout the entire war—in the ghetto, the camps, the prison cells, and the various houses along the way—she always woke up at the slightest sound and remembered everything. Now she touches the wall, confused. She locates a switch, turns on the light, and breathes with relief: she's in the SS man's apartment.

She looks around but the things she finds are ordinary, boring: shoes on shoe trees, a gramophone, a few records, framed family pictures, a photography manual, an old map of Europe, and some stale ginger cake.

She puts on *The Barber of Seville* and takes the cake back to bed.

She's imagined the end of the war many times. Envisioned herself standing eye to eye with a Gestapo officer or an SS man. The one who slapped her because she looked at him. The one who hung her on the hook. Who waved her to the right with a careless, sloppy gesture. She saw herself watching their fear as she meted out justice. She even thought those words: "mete out justice"—but what exactly might that mean? Was she supposed to kill them? By herself? She doesn't even know how to fire a gun. Was someone supposed to hand her a rifle? Show her how to pull the trigger? Was she supposed to watch the body lying on the ground, the convulsions, the blood, perhaps the guts spilling out?

Iza, that's unsightly, her father would say.

She imagines her highly cultured father standing next to her in the military hospital.

Nu, sestra? Well, nurse?

Nu, otets? Well, father?

She wouldn't have to ask for a rifle. Or how to pull the trigger.

All that was needed was a short answer to a short, simple question.

It would have been enough to say: The one behind me. That one with the towel over his eyes . . . And one more, in the corner . . . Can you believe he never once groaned when I changed his bandages? And there's an entire room next door, on the other side of the wall . . .

Iza, her father would whisper, that's enough.

What do you mean that's enough, what do you mean? Didn't he summon you to the trains, as a specialist who knew German? Didn't he shoot my husband's mother at Pawiak? Didn't he . . .

Hush . . . Her father would raise both arms, appalled at how loudly his daughter was talking, and at her strange, high-pitched, quarrelsome voice. I understand what you're saying, but where did you get that voice? And how can people be shot without being tried in a court?

Her father's indignation and the idea of a trial for SS men strike her as highly amusing.

We found them, don't you worry, she says, delighted. What of it? Feeling sorry?

That's the first conversation she's had with her father since he left to explain everything to the Germans . . .

It's the first of many she will have with all of them in her stylish home on Mount Carmel.

135

Ebensee

At the former Polish consulate they're doling out soup.
People stop by, drink their soup, and move on. When
asked where they're going they wave their hands vaguely
toward the east or in the opposite direction.

Izolda stops by every day. She stands at the entrance
and asks anyone wearing stripes: Mauthausen? She drinks
her soup, then returns to the apartment in the evening.
The next morning she's back: Mauthausen?

It's evening. On her way home it starts to rain. Her
priceless bicycle might get wet, so she quickly ducks
inside the nearest entrance. Some men are standing there
dressed in camp clothes and speaking Polish.

She asks where they came from.

Ebensee.

Oh, in that case excuse me. She takes hold of the han-
dlebar and turns to leave.

What camp are you looking for? the men ask.

Mauthausen.

What address did you use for your letters?

Mauthausen, block AKZ.

Well, that's Ebensee—it's a subcamp. What's the
name?

It would be stupid if she fainted now, she thinks, and
leans on the bike for support.

Pawlicki . . . she whispers. Tall . . . very straight and
tall . . . and blond . . . She's afraid that the men will say:

We don't know anyone like that. Or else: Pawlicki—yes, he was there. They'll say *was*, so she speaks quickly, all in one breath, so she won't hear their answer.

I know Pawlicki, one of the men cuts her off.

What do you mean, you know him . . . Tall? Straight? Blond?

Please, lady, the man says. There's no reason to be afraid. He's alive.

The Bridge

Mauthausen is in American hands and Vienna is occupied by the Russians. The border crossing is at Enns, both sides of the bridge are occupied by soldiers of the victorious armies.

She approaches the Soviet sentry and tells him she's trying to get to her husband. He orders her back. If you know what's good for you, he repeats several times, you better go back, because I'll shoot.

She climbs on a truck—*sadis!* Have a seat! The drunken officers with Austrian girls on their laps call for her to get in, but the trip is a short one since they don't have passes. The whole group staggers over to the guardhouse, the sentry gives them a canister of vodka, and tells them to wait for the captain.

The captain stumbles in soon afterward. He checks how much is left in the canister and asks what's going on.

My husband's in the camp . . . she begins. We survived the war . . . Now we're so close but not allowed to meet. Can you understand?

Not allowed, *da, da,* I understand, the captain confirms and bites into the blini a soldier has placed in front of him.

Tell me, she says with a charming smile. Why can't life be like in a film?

And how would it be in a film? The captain dips his blini into the melted butter and waits for her to answer.

In a film I would tell you my story, you would be moved, you would speak with the sentry, and I would walk onto the bridge.

Yes, that would be a beautiful film . . . The captain stops eating. He thinks for a moment, blini in hand, a warm yellow stream of butter dripping toward his sleeve. But I'll tell you a real film. When the front was in Russia, we stopped near my village . . . maybe five kilometers away. I wanted to say goodbye to my wife and to my mother, but our commander said: You're not going anywhere, the war isn't over yet. And when the war was over, you know what? The captain leans across the table, as if he wanted to confess an unusually important secret. My village was no longer there. My mother, my wife, the whole village . . . Can you understand? So you're not going anywhere either. I didn't get to say goodbye and you're not getting to say hello, there won't be any film.

The officers are silent. The captain stands up from behind the table. He signals for her to follow him to the storeroom. *Nu* . . . The captain wears high boots, with a revolver on his belt. He staggers a bit. The rancid butter makes him burp. He points to the camp bed, inviting her: You wanted a film . . .

She places her bag and jacket on the bed. Just a minute, she says, I'll be right back.

The same soldiers who stopped the truck are sitting outside the barracks. She prefers one drunken captain to an entire sober patrol and returns to the storeroom. The captain is lying on the bed, snoring loudly.

She spends the night on the floor, her head resting on one of the captain's boots. In the morning she goes back to the crossing. The officer on duty is one of the merry group from the truck. He greets her like an old friend, gives a signal, and the sentry looks the other way.

She steps onto the bridge.

The American side also has a sentry.

My husband . . . she says in English.

The American listens politely, says: *Oh, yes,* and points to the Soviet side.

No, she says. *My husband* is there—and points to the American side.

Yes, yes—the American soldier pushes her away and points to the bridge.

No, no, Mauthausen is there . . .

The sentry calls someone.

An older officer with salt-and-pepper hair comes over.

He happens to be an army doctor.

He happens to be an American Jew from New York.

America

She tells both men, the one who let her off the bridge and his younger colleague (who is Irish), about the war.

Ghetto—trains—Aryan side—Gestapo—Auschwitz . . .

The older man sighs, and with each sigh he gives her another serving of powdered eggs, alternating with beef out of a tin and pieces of halva. The younger man asks about the balance of forces at Umschlagplatz in the ghetto and specifically how many Germans were there. And how many Jews? So why didn't you defend yourselves? Oh, come on, there's always something to fight with. If you really want to.

The older man understands how terrible it must have been, but: Let me tell you something, lady. This could only happen in Europe. It would be unthinkable in the States. No one would ever go along with it . . .

With what? she asks.

With the trains, the transports . . . No Jewish community in the States would ever allow it.

So they would shoot a few people as an example. And then they'd hang the leader of the community on a hook, like this (she gets up and shows the Americans how the leader of the community would hang on a hook), and then they'd ask if he'd rather have more people shot or sent away on the trains . . . And the ghetto would be . . . Where do Jews live in New York?

Listen, lady, says the American whose grandmother emigrated from Grajewo and whose grandfather came from Maków Mazowiecki. I'm trying to tell you: in the States, in New York, no one would agree to any ghetto in the first place.

Well. Maybe you're right . . .

She falls silent. The sun is rising and she has to make it to Mauthausen.

The Meeting

She climbs up a steep mountain path. She looks at the meadows in the valley, the roses in the gardens, the green window shutters, the white church tower, and the azure sky.

Around a curve she sees some men in camp stripes sitting on rocks. They're smoking cigarettes, turning their faces to the sun. They call out to her: *Kim maydele, kim tsu mir* . . .

What language is that?

Yiddish?!

Come, little girl, come to me—*Kim tsu mir* . . .

That loud, in Yiddish?

She speeds up, hoping they won't follow her. Hoping that no one heard them. Her face breaks out in a sweat, she feels her heart pounding. ("How many times does a heart beat per minute? That depends on whether a person is afraid or not.") A group of women are heading downhill wearing thick woolen skirts, with embroidered traditional waistcoats. *Grüß Gott*—they smile at her nicely. *Grüß Gott*, she responds, recovering her wits. She fixes her blouse, which is wet at the back and under her arms. She smoothes out the white knitted gloves she wore on the train to keep her hands clean. The war is over, she thinks. I'm going to meet my husband. This is the last leg of my journey and it would be silly to lose my mind now.

The path narrows, dwarf mountain pines appear on the slopes.

She sees something that looks like a barracks.

A voice asks her who she's looking for.

I'll take you, says the voice. All she sees is her tennis shoes covered with dust and gravel passing underfoot. She's sitting on the frame of a bicycle. The bicycle stops at the entrance to the barracks. Inside is a long corridor. She walks down the corridor. Someone turns the handle, the door opens, she stops on the threshold. A blond boy is lying in bed, his face is flushed, probably from a fever. A few men are standing nearby, and sitting at the foot of the bed is her husband. He's wearing shorts, without a shirt. Resting his suntanned hands on his knees. He glances up . . . He looks at her. The person who brought her gives a sign, the men leave the room, and the sick boy closes the door. Shayek goes to her and embraces her, slowly, very carefully . . .

She waits.

In just a moment she's going to feel this enormous joy, she imagines. I'm sure I'm going to be very happy.

She doesn't feel joy.

She isn't happy.

She doesn't feel anything, nothing at all.

It's because I'm wearing gloves, she thinks.

She pulls off her gloves behind his back and tosses them to the ground. She strokes him. He's warm. Is that all? She's filled with bitterness. It isn't fair. She's found her husband and she doesn't feel any joy whatsoever.

Shayek untangles her hands.

I have to go out, he says. Just for a moment, wait here.

She sits on the bed and waits as she is told.

At the door he turns around: I'm just going to say you're here.

Say to whom?

To Liesl, says Shayek. I'll just run down . . . It won't take long, wait.

The men come back inside.

Do you know where he ran off to? one of them asks.

Yes. To Liesl.

And you're not upset?

No, why?

She's not bad looking, Liesl, the man says. She's young. A war widow. She kept your husband fed, cured him of pneumonia.

That's very noble. I'm grateful to her . . . Do you know what they called our prison in Vienna—its nickname, I mean? Liesl.

You're a sensible woman, the man acknowledges. He looks through the open door. Your husband's back already . . . It seems he has a present for you.

Souvenir

What about my father? her husband asks.

He's gone.

And Halina?

She's gone.

Your mother?

I don't know. I had a dream . . . I was on a train and my mother was standing on the platform. The steps were too high and she couldn't get in. I wanted to help her, but then the train started. Mama called out: Just go on, don't worry about me!—and she pulled a hood over her head. I'd never seen that hood before. The train was going faster and faster, Mama was getting smaller and smaller, and next she didn't have a face. I woke up and told Nicole that I'd just spoken to my mother for the last time.

Shayek doesn't ask who Nicole is, so she doesn't explain.

They're sitting in a clearing, on a hill. Down below they can see the barracks and, a little farther on, the town.

She counts all the ones who aren't there: his father, mother, sisters, nephew, in-laws, her mother, father, friends—Hala and Basia . . .

She folds down one finger at a time—first on one hand, then the other. Each palm turns into a fist. She stares at her hands.

She says: We're here, you and I are still here. She straightens out the index and middle fingers of her right hand, so that they look like *V* for victory or rabbit ears in a shadow theater for children. I had faith that you would survive. I prayed . . . I was absolutely certain, even though you had those three horrible spades right next to you.

What three horrible spades? her husband asks.

Terenia said it meant you had to keep an eye out, because a dangerous person was lying in wait.

Hartmann! her husband shouts. That had to be him, the meanest kapo in the whole camp. It couldn't be anybody else.

Did he get away?

Are you kidding . . . That reminds me, I have a present.

He reaches for a little package tied with an elegant ribbon (from Liesl's braid, she guesses . . . or else her box of chocolates). He removes the paper. Inside the box, lying on a silver piece of foil taken from a packet of cigarettes, is a longish, dark object.

Don't you recognize it? her husband laughs. Those three spades! The Germans ran away, but the oven was still burning in the crematorium.

The oven was still burning, her husband repeats a little absentmindedly.

Or maybe it wasn't. Maybe we lit it especially for Hartmann. Well? Tell me you appreciate it. This comes from his skull. I managed to save a piece specially for you.

What about the rest of him? she asks, and wonders if she would be that indifferent if it were the skull of *Aufseherin* Piontek.

They took him apart, he says, shrugging his shoulders. Broke him up into presents.

You don't like it . . . Shayek is visibly disappointed. Would you rather have some chocolate? I'll bring you some.

He stands up, but then remembers something.

Listen . . . he lowers his voice, although there's no one around. I didn't tell you the most important thing. They think I'm Polish. I don't know if you understand . . .

I understand.

Let's keep it that way, he says. Let's make sure no one ever finds out about us. Ever. No one. I don't know if you understand me.

I understand you very well.

Shayek climbs a short distance down the slope and looks back. She's sitting with her arms wrapped around her knees. Her husband isn't looking at her face. He's looking at her legs showing under her skirt and the white triangle of underwear between her thighs.

What are you doing sitting like that! he shouts. Straighten your legs and sit decently!

She straightens her legs.

My legs no longer belong to me, she thinks, surprised. Their rightful owner has returned and he can tell them to do what he wants.

She carefully adjusts her skirt. She stretches out on the warm moss—with joy and unbounded relief.

The Return

They take over the apartment on Operngasse. The SS man's shoes fit her husband perfectly, they set their own pictures in the frames, she studies the map of Europe to find the way back to Poland.

She marks out the route, but her husband says: Hold off on that, it's really nice here in Vienna.

They walk along the Danube, visit museums, drop by the offices of the Polish representation. They meet Stefa's friend, the typist from the Ostbahn, who gave Izolda the patent-leather high heels. Stefa's already in Australia, her friend knows the address. Izolda receives a letter from Australia, just a few lines: "I saw your mother in Warsaw, she wanted to leave, but didn't have any place to go. She died in a basement in early August, during the first days of the uprising. I don't know which basement, I wanted to find out, but then they sent us to the transit camp." In a PS, Stefa writes that she's been accepted at the university to study psychology (they decided to count her first year from before the war), and asks if Izolda received the package she sent by registered mail. The package does arrive a few days later with a stamp from the Soviet customs office: *provereno*—verified. A small box wrapped in heavy gray paper, with a couple of bars of chocolate and Izolda's compact. The one Shayek gave her at their engagement party. (They were all there: both mothers, both fathers, his sisters with their husbands, little Szymuś . . . No, Szymuś wasn't there. He started to whine and Tusia put him to bed early.) The silver compact with the beautiful engraving, the one the Jewish policeman didn't take at Umschlagplatz. The one the fortune-teller at the Saxon Gardens used to read the first letter of her real name. (It was in the autumn, Izolda was sitting on a bench. A woman she didn't know approached her and said that for five zlotys she would read her name and her fortune from a mirror. Izolda handed her the compact. The woman wiped off the powder and peered into the mirror for several moments. I don't know, she said at last, you have a long, difficult name that starts with the letter *I* . . . Back then she hadn't been Izolda for a long time: she was Marynia. She had her identity card, the park was empty, the woman wasn't a threat—but nevertheless Izolda jumped up, grabbed the compact, and ran off as fast as she could.) The same that she left with Stefa before her last trip to Vienna—with the tobacco, the Count, and Janka Tempelhof.

Let's go back, she repeats. It's time to find out . . .

Find out what? asks Shayek.

About Lilusia. About Mrs. Krusiewicz. About that basement . . .

Her husband agrees, but first he wants to meet up with the boys. He has to talk with them, say goodbye.

He rides out to Ebensee to see his comrades from the camp who are still there and who don't know what to do next.

He comes back with news: Poland is now communist, a plane arrived for the French prisoners at the camp (his friends believe a plane will arrive for them as well, most likely from America, but somehow it never does), and Liesl's husband came back home, a fairly pleasant man, he was wounded, fortunately not too badly . . .

They travel to Poland.

Her husband insists on living in Łódź. (His father, Mosze Luzer Regensberg, owned a textile mill on Nowomiejska Street called Red and White that manufactured towels and bedding. Of course Shayek is no longer a Regensberg, and no one dares mention Mosze Luzer. Nevertheless, he insists that if they have to go back to Poland, they need to be near the defunct Red and White textile mill.)

She visits a surgeon who removes the Jewish triangle and the Jewish *A* from her arm, leaving a tattooed number like the Aryans had, for a prisoner with a record, a number she can show the whole world in the summer when she wears a short-sleeved dress.

She goes to a photographer and hands him a picture

of a Jew with a beard—Mosze Luzer. She asks if the beard might be removed. It will be hard, says the photographer, but I'll do my best. He creates a negative, retouches the beard, and proudly delivers the prints. Prints that show Shayek's father clean-shaven, the way he was under the windowsill at the honest widow's. Shayek buys an elegant frame, puts the picture inside, and hangs it in a conspicuous place.

She signs up for nursing school.

She gives birth to two daughters. She examines them warily. Each has dark features, but not like hers. The first thing she does is tell her husband they look like him. Which means: not like his father, Mosze Luzer, or her mother, Hinda.

Mrs. Krusiewicz is godmother to the elder daughter and Lilusia to the younger. Both celebrate their first communion on the same day, all excited, in beautiful dresses with charming garlands of fresh lilies of the valley. The girls are very devout, never miss a Sunday Mass—the earliest one, at six in the morning—and on fast days they refuse to drink even water. Now and then they ask about their grandparents. Izolda has different variations of Polish death all prepared: partisans, Katyn, underground university, Warsaw Uprising, but the girls don't pursue matters.

Their life is safe and peaceful, disrupted only by her husband. He comes home from work and says: I saw a woman who looked like Halina. She even had Halina's hair—yellowish blond, but not ugly. I followed her off the tram. I stared at her awhile and then said: Excuse me, I thought maybe my sister . . . You know—maybe she's alive but doesn't know that we are?

They visit the apartment on Pomorska Street where his family lived before the war. They find the name REGENS-BERG on an old list of tenants by the entrance. (I told you . . . her husband whispers.) They climb the first flight of stairs. The door is open, the apartment is being used as a clinic. Patients are waiting in the front hall, name tags of doctors are fixed to the dining-room and bedroom doors, his father's office is now the reception. Is Mrs. Regensberg here? her husband asks. Is she a nurse or a doctor? asks the receptionist. She's my sister, her husband says. We . . . I'm so sorry to bother you.

He comes back from work . . . He saw his father again, and with his beard, too. He followed him . . .

Why should that person be alive, and with his black Jewish beard, while my father isn't? My father could be here . . . And my mother could be . . .

If what? She sets down her coffee cup and looks at her husband.

If they had stayed at the widow's.

She threw them out! On a scorching-hot day, when the sun was at its peak!

Because you were at Pawiak. The woman became scared, that's not so hard to understand. How did you end up at Pawiak anyway?

I went to say goodbye to Basia Gajer, she explains for the umpteenth time.

Exactly, says her husband. Did you really have to do that?

Do you seriously think—she raises her voice—that your parents died because of me?

Keep it down, her husband whispers. The building isn't very soundproof—God forbid the neighbors might overhear what they're talking about.

Józefów

Jurek Szwarcwald drops in. He's wearing an officer's uniform and is happy and proud because he won election to the Sejm as a representative from Pomerania. He'd been in charge of a propaganda brigade, agitating and writing political plays. The heroes were all peasants, workers, and soldiers, while the villains were landowners and members of the reactionary underground. The plays were performed in army theaters, with 100 percent attendance. His work was appreciated: the minister himself awarded him the Order of Polonia Restituta.

Jurek Szwarcwald is there on business: he is selling his properties. As an honest communist he doesn't want to be the owner of four summer houses in Józefów.

(Summer in Józefów . . .

waking up in the dark, when the shutters are still closed . . .

sunlight peeking through the little hearts carved in the shutters . . .

walks in the sandy glades . . .

the oak tree in the glade, so big and spreading, with cracked bark and so many acorns . . . It's at least a hundred years old, said Fräulein Maria, but what's that for an oak tree . . .

Fräulein Maria Hunkert, Jurek Szwarcwald's governess . . . after her own child died she became a wet nurse to little Jurek . . .

acorn soldiers, acorn beads . . .

evenings on the veranda . . . the kerosene lantern made of white majolica painted with colorful flowers and the slender, tall glass . . . the bright circle of light in the middle of the table . . .)

Her husband would like to tell Jurek what he thinks of communism.

She cuts him off, she doesn't want to make their guest

feel bad. Thanks to Jurek she found work in the typhus ward and thanks to him she met Bolek. If it weren't for the typhus ward they wouldn't have rescued her from Umschlagplatz. And if it weren't for Bolek . . .

A man comes who's interested in buying the patch of forest and the summer houses. He notes that there aren't many trees and that the houses are small, wooden, without running water.

Jurek agrees with him completely and signs a piece of paper.

The new owner of the summer houses and the woods hands Jurek the money and leaves.

So, now we've taken care of Józefów, says Jurek Szwarcwald.

Work

She works as a dispatcher in an emergency-services center. On a few occasions she refuses to send an ambulance to a party secretary. She very patiently explains that ambulances cannot be dispatched in cases that aren't life-threatening, but they fire her anyway.

She gives up nursing.

She helps her husband with his textile business. He owns several looms but unfortunately they start having problems with the yarn supply.

They switch to plastic mats and doilies. The pattern is cut onto a stencil that is covered with material and baked in an oven. The doilies look handmade and the clients like them, but they start having problems with the polyvinyl chloride supply.

They switch to gold belts for dresses. Their clients like that even more, but the revenue office puts a duty on gold foil, the problems keep getting worse.

Travel Document

They summon her husband to the *milicja*.

It's not about taxes, duties, or gold foil. A few yellowed papers are lying on the officer's desk. The officer slides them toward her husband and gestures politely for him to read.

One paper is the birth certificate of Mosze Luzer Regensberg. The second is a marriage certificate for Mosze Luzer and Regina Rutenberg. The third is an order for the firm Red and White.

Shayek touches the cards very carefully, as though he were afraid they might fall apart in his hands, but the officer reassures him: That's good, prewar paper, Mr. Pawlicki, it's been through a lot. Well? the officer asks, with a sigh. When are we going back to our real names? Don't you think it's about time, Mr. Regensberg?

They go to the passport office. If they list their nationality as "Jewish" they'll be issued passports within a week.

They list their nationality as Jewish and are given cards marked "*Dokument Podróży*." The "travel document" informs in several languages that the bearer is not a Polish citizen: *Vladelets nastoyashchego dokumenta . . . le titulaire de ce titre . . .*

Mrs. Krusiewicz has passed away, they say goodbye to one person: Kazimiera Szubert.

Lilusia sits in her armchair, her twisted hands clutching a walking stick. She scans the travel document with slight disgust. She thinks for a moment . . . probably about what to give them as a farewell gift.

The medallion—she asks suddenly. With the Mother of God . . . Do you still have it?

I have to confess I don't.

You don't have the medallion? With the Mother of God? She had a tear . . . Not very large, but it was there—right on her cheek. Do you happen to remember where you lost it?

I do. I lost it in Auschwitz.

In Auschwitz . . . Lilusia repeats. In Auschwitz, I see . . .

Don't cry, she reminds Lilusia. Don't you know that we mustn't cry?

Walls

They're back in Vienna.

Her daughters study at the university, her husband has a shop selling jeans. She helps him out, taking care of the clients. She hands one young man sixteen pairs, he tries each of them on and finally buys the seventeenth. She wishes him a good holiday and wonders if it's possible to escape from a jeans shop. It is possible, but where to?

They return home, tired. Without taking off his coat, her husband switches on the record player—a piercing, mournful Jewish song. He drops into the armchair, props his head on his hands, and stares at the photographs that hang, enlarged, on every wall. Hela is wearing a pink hat and a summer dress with large pink flowers—the photographer painted the cheerful pastel colors onto the old picture. Luckily Halina is in black and white, so her overly yellow hair isn't too conspicuous. Shayek's father appears in two versions: with and without beard. Tusia is lost in thought, calm as always, her hair combed smooth and parted, with a black velvet bow below her white collar. And her son, Szymuś, more serious than his six years. And Zosia, the prettiest of the sisters, whom she never met, the sister who left for Lwów and never got in touch.

What are you doing sitting there? she asks her husband. Why are you staring at them? When they were alive you always quarreled.

That's not true, he says, I didn't quarrel with them at all.

What are you saying? The first time I went to your house you were very put out with Halina.

I said I was sorry. And—you may not remember—I even praised her soup . . .

Because I asked you to. We were sitting at the table and you said: This soup is delicious, did you make it? Halina smiled and said: I'm glad you like it. I whispered to you: Say something nice about the soup.

There, you see. I made up with all of them and so I'm allowed to be despondent. I want to be despondent, so leave me alone.

Her younger daughter meets a boy, a Jew from Sweden. She abandons her Polish love, the architecture student Sławek B., and goes on holiday with the Swede. They spend it on a kibbutz and when she comes back she informs her parents that she's moving to Israel.

The country is in a state of war, she explains to her daughter.

It's my country, her daughter says.

They'll draft your husband.

So? It's his army and his country.

He might die! Don't you understand that they could kill him?

So they'll kill him. He'll die for his country.

During the war I was the same age you are now, she tells her daughter. And there was no cause more important to me than my husband. The whole world could fall apart as long as he survived, and you?

And I have more important causes, her daughter says. Causes worth dying for.

Izolda remembers her conversation with Nicole—about her children not dying, guilty of nothing but . . . It must have been an evil hour when she said those words, she thinks, terrified.

The Letter

First one daughter and then the next move to Israel, leaving them all alone in the Viennese apartment.

Nothing much changes in their lives.

She gets up first. She puts coffee in the espresso pot and sets two cups on the table. She wakes her husband. They go to work, sell jeans. They come back. She cooks dinner. Her husband sits in the armchair.

Why don't you say anything? she asks.

He says he doesn't want to.

You're thinking about them again.

No, he says, I'm thinking about myself.

And what are you thinking?

I'm wondering.

Wondering what?

He doesn't answer. But she knows: he's wondering whether he ought to have survived the war. Why he? Out of his entire family? Why? With what right?

She knows exactly why he survived: it was because of her. The Americans liberated him, but they weren't the ones who saved him. Her love, her thoughts, her strength, and her prayers kept him alive.

(Don't tell him that he survived because of you, Lilusia advised her. Don't ever tell him that . . .)

Our daughters wouldn't be here if you hadn't survived . . . Our daughters have your sisters' faces. Who would have your sisters' faces if it weren't for you?

He doesn't answer, but she knows anyway: now he'll think about his sisters.

She goes to bed. Her husband gets up from the armchair and sits down at the desk.

Undoubtedly he's sending one more ad to some paper in Israel or America or the Ukraine: "Seeking my sister Zosia Regensberg, nineteen years old, daughter of Regina and Mosze Luzer Regensberg. Last seen in Lwów . . ."

Undoubtedly he'll stop writing . . . He'll hesitate . . . He'll cross out "nineteen" and start to count . . . Undoubtedly he'll be surprised . . . Sixty? How is that possible?

She gets up first.

She goes to the kitchen.

She reaches for the coffee, the coffee canister is on the shelf, over the sewing machine.

On top of the machine, just below the label "Singer," is a folded sheet of paper.

She pours coffee into the espresso pot, places two cups on the table, puts on her glasses, and unfolds the paper. It's a letter to her. Her husband informs her that he's going away, forever. "I'm leaving and won't be back. I'll pay you fifty dollars a week. I'll also pay the rent and the telephone, on the condition the bills aren't extravagant. I wish you all the best . . ."

A Book

She likes Israel.

People aren't shy about giving advice: in the bus they tell her where to get off, in the shop what to buy, at the post office which card to send for New Year and which for Rosh Hashanah. Everyone wants to know where she was during the war and everyone wants to tell her something. In Tel Aviv she asks how to find the bus station and a woman tells her all about herself and then about her husband, who was at the Hotel Polski . . . She interrupts the woman: It was because of Hotel Polski that I ended up in Pawiak. In Pawiak? the woman cries out. My brother was in Pawiak. They stand on the street and after an hour she asks: So, where is the bus station?

She listens to strangers' tales with genuine sympathy: one person hid in a basement, another in a root cellar, an attic, a closet, a haystack. They lived through terrible things, but their experiences weren't so varied. Unlike hers.

She grows more and more convinced that her life is a great subject for a book. Or even a film.

She's lucky: the Americans are making a film at the Jerusalem airport about a hijacked Israeli plane, starring Elizabeth Taylor.

She rides out to the airport. They don't want to let her in. She explains to the officer in charge of security that she has to speak at once to the actress. The officer wants to know what about. About life—a life that will make a great film, Taylor could play the lead. The officer looks at the number on her arm. My father died there . . . he says. There, you see, she says—and I stepped right up to Dr. Mengele.

The officer discourages her from talking to the movie star and advises her to start with a book instead: You need to find a good writer.

She works hard, taking care of old people. She is patient. To the professor who fled Germany after Kristall-nacht she speaks in a low voice, one syllable at a time (he's a little deaf and can't hear long words or high pitches). To the lawyer who spent the war in the Soviet Union she speaks of Poland. How often did they change your bedding? he asks. Where do you mean? You know . . . in Auschwitz. Not very often, right?

She takes a holiday once a year, always in the sum-mer. She spends it looking for a good writer. The person shouldn't be young, should know what war is like, what love is like.

She starts with a writer in Israel, not young.

The writer agrees with her, her life would be a great subject for a book, but she has to write it herself. It's not that hard, he assures her, I'll give you an example. You're riding to Vienna with the tobacco. You place your black lacquered suitcase on the shelf, a moment later an SS man enters the compartment—tall and very handsome. He places his yellow pigskin suitcase beside your black one and sits across from you. Maybe he stands next to the window. He smokes a cigarette . . . He's clearly waiting for someone . . . The writer stops. And then what? she asks. How am I supposed to know? the writer answers, impatient. You're the one who's supposed to know, not me, as it is I've already said a lot. Izolda insists: At least tell me what he has in the yellow suitcase. And who he's waiting for next to the window . . . That's precisely the secret, says the writer. That's what has to be unraveled, that's the essence of literature . . .

From time to time her husband calls their daughters from Vienna.

Papa called, her daughter says.

And?

Everything's okay. He feels fine, the jeans are selling well . . .

Did he ask about me?

No.

Did you say anything about me?

He didn't ask.

The next writer lives in France.

She tells him about her extraordinary life . . . The Doctor? he cries out. I know him! He hid me and my wife. And a translator of German poetry. You could forgive him . . .

Forgive?! He led me on, cheated me, robbed me of hope. I should forgive him because he saved someone else?

The Doctor saved me, the writer repeats.

(He won't write about Izolda. He's interested in his own stories, not other people's.)

She offers an author in Poland a nice honorarium. The woman writes a book but it does not meet Izolda's expectations. Not enough feeling. Not enough love, loneliness, and tears. Not enough heart. Not enough words. Not enough of everything, simply not enough.[*]

Sochaczewski

Her husband has had a heart attack.

His coronary disease is getting worse.

His depression is getting deeper.

He agrees to spend a holiday together.

Concentration-camp survivors can receive free treatment at German sanatoriums every two years. A designated doctor examines them and if the illness is the result of Nazi persecution they receive a referral. Not every illness is the result of Nazi persecution, for instance heart disease is not. But depression is. The doctor prescribes a change of environment (that's worked wonders in similar cases) and they travel to the sanatorium.

The resort is in a park on a lake, from their windows they can see the mountains—it's beautiful. They go for

---

[*] I wrote about the "author in Poland" and Izolda R. in a piece entitled "A Novel for Hollywood," which may be regarded as a draft for this book. —HK

walks. They ride in a boat. In the afternoon they sit on the café terrace and play cards—"smart rummy" that her father brought back from Sopot. (He went there several times a year, in the casino he tried out his new system of winning at roulette. The system was never perfected, but he liked rummy and the whole family enjoyed playing.)

They return to Vienna.

Her husband feels ill, the doctor confirms pneumonia.

Her husband is in the hospital. He sleeps a lot. He wakes up and says: Please, go and see Sochaczewski. Tell him where I am, have him come and visit.

Who's Sochaczewski? she asks.

You don't know? Huma's husband.

And who is Huma?

You don't know that either? Aunt Huma, my mother's sister!

And where do these Sochaczewskis live?

Good God, where do you think they live? Right nearby, on Pomorska Street.

There isn't any Pomorska Street here. This is Vienna.

Vienna, her husband repeats, and starts to cry.

Listen, her husband says, clearly put out. You haven't been living at home lately, can I know why?

Because you didn't want to be with me.

What kind of nonsense is that? I didn't want to?

You left a letter . . . It was on the sewing machine.

I remember something . . . Are you sure it was to you? All right, so this is Vienna—her husband refuses to give up—still you could have called Sochaczewski. Like I told you. Just ask if he's a rabbi yet. And where he is, because we could visit him.

I didn't know that Sochaczewski wanted to become a rabbi . . .

You never know anything, her husband says, irritated. It's his dream to become a rabbi. He spends his whole life with the Torah and dreams that somewhere in the countryside, in a quiet little town . . .

And I'm supposed to find out where that is. The quiet little town where Sochaczewski is a rabbi, is that what you're after?

Now you've got it—he calms down. Finally. That's not so hard, is it?

You look so pretty, he says, brightening up at the sight of his younger daughter. I've been waiting and waiting for you. Didn't you bring little Szymuś with you?

Beseder

Something's wrong with her eyesight because of macular degeneration. There are two types: wet and dry. Laser treatment is available for the wet type, but she has the dry type. All she can see is the outlines of figures, very blurred, as though in a fog.

Something's wrong with her lower back and she can't walk.

Something's wrong with the cartilage in her knees, it's probably going.

Her hands start to shake. Her legs and feet shake, too, and so do her toes. Except that each part shakes for a different reason: Her feet from Parkinson's and her toes because of something in her brain. Or from a muscle disease that can't be treated.

She's turned the television on, though she doesn't see the picture. She's turned on the sound, though she doesn't know Hebrew. Her Russian caretaker tells her what's going on. Oh, she says, something happened, people running. Was there a bombing? Yes, there is an ambulance. Look, it's nearby, right here by our beach . . . *Gospodi*—my God, they're showing our restaurant.

Izolda gropes for her walking frame, lifts herself out of the armchair, and through the thick, milky fog tries to make out the ruins of the restaurant.

They're showing a girl, her caretaker reports. A woman is crying, must be the mother. No, not the mother, oh— now it's the mother . . .

The telephone rings. *Babcia?*—"grandmother" is one of the few Polish words her granddaughters know. *Ani beseder.*

She sighs with relief: *beseder*—"fine"—is one of the few Hebrew words she knows.

Everything okay? her Russian caretaker asks: *Vsyo v poryadke? Vsyo beseder?*

The Monument

Her younger daughter is going to Poland (Sławek B., her great first love, is building a monument and is asking for help).

The monument will be in Łódź, at the train station that used to be called Radegast. That was where the Jews of Łódź boarded the trains bound for Chełmno, Auschwitz, and other camps.

Her younger daughter asks her about the Łódź ghetto (you saw it, after all, from the tram).

People wore yellow stars.

I know that, her daughter says.

The streets were deserted . . . almost empty . . .

Why? her daughter asks. There were two hundred thousand people there . . .

Exactly, she agrees. I thought it was strange too. And the few who were on the streets stood there and looked at me. What am I saying . . . they were staring at the tram.

Her younger daughter studies the pictures taken by the photographer Henryk Ross. He worked in the Łódź Judenrat and so was allowed to carry a camera and film. Ross buried three thousand negatives that survived the war. He was a witness at the Eichmann trial. The judge showed him pictures and asked what was on them, and the witness explained. For instance, what is on photograph T/224, which shows children looking for something in the ground. The witness explained that the children were looking for potatoes. Frozen, rotten potatoes were chlorinated and buried by order of the authorities. The children knew this, they dug up the potatoes and ate them. Photograph T/225 shows people who died of hunger. Some died bloated, others emaciated, the witness explained. T/226 shows people waiting to be deported. T/227 the same. T/229 the same. Two or three hundred people standing in line to board the trains. And T/233 shows a family heading to the trains— father, mother, and two children. Deportation meant death, the witness added. Deportation where? asked the attorney general. To Chełmno, answered the witness. The prosecutor wanted to know how photograph T/234 was taken. Actually that photo was taken in Radegast Station itself. Some acquaintances who worked there smuggled the witness in and locked him inside a cement warehouse. He stayed there from six in the morning to seven in the evening. He heard the shouts. He saw how they shot the people who didn't want to board. He saw the train pull away full of people. He saw everything through a small opening in the wall. Through that opening he took photographs T/234 and several others. T/236 shows where the ghetto stopped and the road to Radegast began, and on T/237 you can see people walking down that road. The judge asked the defense attorney Dr. Servatius if he had any questions for the witness. Dr. Servatius did not. The judge thanked Henryk Ross for his testimony.

Izolda's younger daughter travels to Poland. Together with Sławek B. they look at the wooden station building, the tracks, which are also genuine (trains are using them to this day), and a genuine freight car. Sławek B. wants to erect oversized *matzevas* with the names of the camps and a tall, broken column, which in Jewish symbolism stands for a life cut short. On the column will be the Fifth Commandment: Thou shalt not kill. Between the station and the Fifth Commandment he proposes a tunnel showing what the Jews left behind. Glasses, apartment keys, pictures, and names, tens of thousands of names. Izolda's daughter buys a notebook, in case she has to take notes. Sławek's wife, Marysia, picks them up from the train station when they return from Łódź. The table is set for dinner, their son is slicing tomatoes for the salad. Marysia sits down to talk with Izolda's daughter. Her son calls her into the kitchen to make a dressing for the salad.

She keeps running back and forth between kitchen and table. While in the kitchen she tries some food—maybe the dressing or the meat—to check if it's ready. She swallows too quickly and chokes. The ambulance arrives. The doctors try to revive her. Marysia dies.

Armchair

If it weren't for the tobacco and Vienna (this thought will haunt her more and more persistently), she would have died in the basement together with her mother.

If she hadn't escaped from Guben, she would have died of typhus together with Janka Tempelhof.

If her younger daughter hadn't gone to Poland . . .

If there hadn't been dinner . . .

If Marysia hadn't checked . . .

If the monument hadn't been . . .

If the Łódź ghetto hadn't been . . .

The Sochaczewskis

Izolda's younger daughter writes the names of the Sochaczewski family in her notebook. It was a large family and inside the tunnel they appear on several different lists. Mayer and Pesa, their daughters Tola and Golda, and their grandson Itzek, only a few months old, went to

Chełmno. They were followed by Ryvka with her brother Moszek, her sister Ruchla, and two twin daughters, Chana and Luba. And Dawid also went with his three grandchildren, Rochna, Chaya, and Dawid.

Izolda's younger daughter doesn't know and will never find out if one of those men was Aunt Huma's husband. And if he was a rabbi. And if he managed to settle in a nice, quiet little town.

The Party

For her birthday Izolda's daughters prepare an enormous banquet. Everyone is there—the daughters, granddaughters, son-in-law—only the soldier granddaughter is missing. They didn't grant her leave and now she's guarding some border post. She lets Palestinians into Israel. Every Palestinian assures the granddaughter that he's going to work, and she has to guess which one will work and which will blow himself up along with a bus, a market, or a restaurant.

Izolda would like to give her granddaughter some advice, not about Palestinians, but in general. She'd also like to advise her granddaughter's colleague, a student assigned to guard the checkpoint with a metal detector. That's the most dangerous work in all Israel, because in case of an attack the guard at the checkpoint is the first to die. Izolda would like to give lots of good advice to everyone at the table—on how to survive. And it would be hard to find a better expert at that. No doubt about it: she is an outstanding specialist at surviving.

She sits in the place of honor.

Everyone is very warm to her, except she doesn't see them and she doesn't understand what they're saying because they're speaking Hebrew. Now and then they realize this and switch to English. She should be able to answer, after all she studied for three whole months. You don't have to speak it perfectly, her grandson encourages her.

On the contrary, she is able to speak perfectly: *High above the city, on a tall column, stood the statue of the Happy Prince* . . .

Oscar Wilde, she adds with pride. I had a wonderful English teacher (she says these words in English), but after three months . . .

She doesn't know how to say "hanged himself "—they didn't cover this topic in their lessons. Maybe it's better, after all Mrs. Szwarcwald's lodger isn't the best subject for a birthday party. Or Mrs. Szwarcwald for that matter. (Poison—how do you say that? She can't remember that either.)

What happened after three months? the grandson asks.

Nothing, the teacher gave up teaching.

That's too bad, says the grandson.

And so—advice. The outstanding specialist at surviving wishes to give her family some valuable pointers. All have been verified on the basis of her rich personal experience.

For instance:

dye your hair,

change your voice,

have a calm, self-assured way of looking,

don't place your bag in a Jewish manner, or wring rags like a Jew, or say Hail Mary like a Jew,

make a deal with God,

make sure you stick exactly to your end of the bargain,

listen to the voice of your daemon,

and . . .

What are you laughing at, *babcia*? her grandson asks.

Once again they're talking in Hebrew. Evidently about Sławek B. and whether her younger daughter should move to Poland. Sławek has asked her to, but she doesn't want to leave her children. Incidentally Izolda's daughter has four daughters of her own—strikingly similar to those other four.

In her thoughts and in Polish Izolda starts adding and subtracting.

Two thousand and five minus nineteen hundred and forty-two . . . add thirty-one . . . makes for how much? Ninety-four? Holy Mother of God, Hela would be that old? So Tusia would be ninety-two . . . And Szymuś, imagine that, a seventy-year-old Szymuś!

איך היה בהודו?
מצוין, אחרי הצבא זה המקום הכי טוב לאדם בעולם.
יש לך תחושה פיזית שאת יכולה לעשות הכל והכל מותר לך...
ומה עם השערות? בלי שער הרגשת יותר חופשייה?
זה מוזר, אבל כן... קשה לי עכשיו לחזור לשערות, ללימודים,
למשמעת. בלילות אני חולמת על הודו...*

She sits at the head of the table. The way her mother
always sat . . . Her father ought to be across from her. Let's
hope he wouldn't go on about women's smiles. Better he
should talk about that new color. And even better—let
him explain how he could possibly have gone to them. To
the Germans! Answering their call!

מה זה הדג הזה?
בטוח מבריכה. כיום מגדלים הכל...
את יודעת לעשות גפילטע פיש? בעצמי פעם עשיתי.
החוכמה היא לפרק את הדג מבלי לשפוך את המרה...
ואחרי זה להקפיד שלא יהיה יותר מדי קמח מצות.†

Why didn't those people want to listen to her?
If her mother hadn't moved out of the gatehouse . . .

* How was India?
   Great. That's the best place on earth for someone who's just finished the army.
   You have this physical sense of being able to do anything and that you're allowed
   to do anything . . .
   What's with the hair? Shaving your head made you feel even freer?
   I know it sounds strange, but it's true . . . It's hard for me to come back—to my
   hair, to studying, discipline. At night I dream about India . . .
† What kind of fish is that?
   I'm sure it's farmed. Everything is farm-raised these days.
   Do you know how to make gefilte fish? I made it once. You have to clean the entire
   fish without spilling the bile . . . And not use too much matzoh meal.

If Halina hadn't trusted a stranger . . .
If her father hadn't gone to the Germans . . .
If the couple hadn't been so loud at the stove . . .
If Janka Tempelhof hadn't stayed in Guben . . .

לא, לא אסע. כבר החלטתי ואל תשאלי אותי יותר שאלות.
את הרי אוהבת אותו.
אני מאוד מבקשת ממך, אל תשאלי שאלות.
היית יכולה להיות קצת אתו וקצת אצלנו עם הבנות.
לא הייתי יכולה. אני מוכרחה להיות שלמה עם הכל. ואני מבקשת ממך...*

And if your Shayek had gone to get his sisters a little
sooner. Couldn't you have prodded him more: Go to your
sisters, they need to get out . . .

Whose voice is that? Is that Hela's husband? He
could have prodded his wife himself. His fair-haired wife
. . . Anyway, Hela isn't the absurd age of ninety—she's
suntanned and pretty, with a long slender neck . . . Her
bronzed skin looks good with light-colored hair. With
hair like that and such blue eyes, couldn't Hela have . . . ?

Shayek asked her not to say anything against his sisters.

She doesn't say anything against them, just asks questions.

She too is allowed to ask a few questions.

---

* No, I'm not going. I've made up my mind and stop asking questions.
   But you love him.
   I said stop asking questions, please.
   You could spend some time with him and some time here with us, with the girls.
   I couldn't. I have to be okay with everything. I'm asking you . . .

Besides, Hela doesn't begrudge her the questions, she just wants to know . . .

What does that Hela want to know now?

What was it like at Pawiak? asks Hela. Did you really turn away . . . ?

After all, Shayek's mother doesn't hold it against her, on the contrary, my daughter-in-law was smart, very smart, only (her mother-in-law asks) couldn't you have . . . I know it would have been hard, but couldn't you have tried to take Halina and her father to Vienna . . . ?

I couldn't, I didn't have money . . .

Maybe I did have money, but that was for him, I had to save him . . .

Him . . . For him . . . He . . .

Remember, don't tell him that he survived because of you . . .

Who is saying that? Lilusia? But Lilusia, it was because of my prayers, my thoughts, my strength, believe me, that was why he survived!

And then what? He left you . . . Your king of hearts wrote you a letter and moved out . . .

Who . . . ? Who's saying that . . . ?

After all, I carried him inside me, like you carry a child. Is it my fault? Is a pregnant woman guilty for having her belly?

על חוף הים הצבנו פסל ענקי מעץ, שהוקדש לידידנו
(הוא טבע בים כשניסה להציל ילד...) מאוחר יותר הצתנו את הפסל.
היה ערב, ים, מוזיקה ואש.
העץ הבוער התחיל להתפרק ולפתע התגלה אדם. כולם קפאו במקומם...
אדם בין הלהבות? מובן מאליו שזה לא היה אדם אמיתי אלא פסלון
מפלסטיק, אך הרושם היה בלתי רגיל.
הנכם מעלים על הדעת? אדם בתוך הלהבות על רקע הים...*

---

* We left a large wooden statue at the beach, dedicated to our friend (he drowned in the sea saving a child . . .). Then we set fire to the statue. It was evening, the sea, there was music, a fire. The burning wood started to fall apart and suddenly a man appeared. Everyone froze: a man in the flames? Of course it wasn't a real man, just a figure made of plastic, but it made an incredible impression. Can you imagine? A man in the flames, with the sea in the background . . .

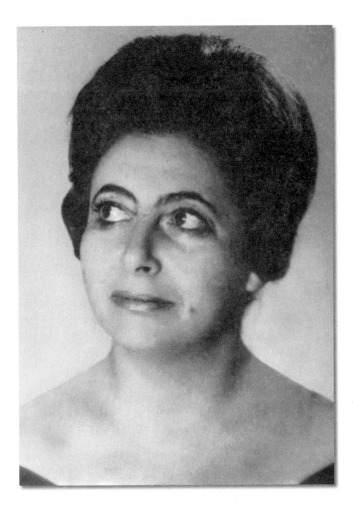

Afterword

One day Hanna Krall learned over the phone that a woman from Israel, whom she didn't know, wanted to have a book about herself. This book was to be written by Krall. She asked the man who called with this news: "Is this woman's life worth writing about?"

Poland's leading author of true-life stories had never written a book to order, but this time she thought the role of ghostwriter could be useful. It was the 1980s, communism was still in force in Poland, and her daughter and son-in-law had emigrated to Canada.

Her dream was to go and visit them there, but she hadn't the money for a ticket.

Some time earlier, the authorities had condemned two of her books to total destruction. In those days, the printers typeset books on metal templates, so the entire typeset text of the first book, all ready for printing, was tossed into the furnace and melted down. And the second book, which had already been printed, was shredded. "They shredded ten thousand books using special knives, dropped from a height like a guillotine," says Krall. She discovered that her book had been shredded alongside the verses of the Russian poet, Osip Mandelstam, who perished in a Soviet camp during the Great Terror in 1938. It seems a collection of his poems had been printed in socialist Poland by mistake, so an immediate decision had been taken to consign it to oblivion.

The authorities had probably determined—rather late in the day—that books by Krall and Mandelstam had the potential of lethal weapons.

The sorrow that Krall diffused in her reportage about communist Poland was more than the authorities could endure.

Clearly, at that time, Krall and her husband's dream of visiting their daughter in Canada had no chance of coming true.

As the fee on offer was equal in value to two plane tickets, she had a meeting with her potential heroine from Israel, whose name was Izolda R.

"Why do you want a book about yourself?" asked Krall.

She said she needed it for a movie. It was to be a major success worldwide, and the movie would be made in Hollywood. She was to be played by Elizabeth Taylor.

Izolda R. believed her life was unusual, her problems were unusual too, and on top of that, she had survived Auschwitz, which should be a selling point for the book.

Krall explained to her that nobody had ever written anything better about Auschwitz than the Polish author Tadeusz Borowski and the Italian author Primo Levi.

"But I was in other places too!" Izolda R. assured her. "I got out of Auschwitz and those other camps. And all for him . . ."

It was the story of a woman whose love for her husband was infinite, and who had saved his life during the war.

Krall commented that Izolda R. would have to pay a Western author, in America for example, ten times more.

"I know," agreed the heroine, "but I haven't the money for American authors. I live off a pension, and to pay you I'll take a job as caregiver for an old woman who's blind and half-deaf, only capable of hearing low-pitched sounds. I talk to her in the voice of a ventriloquist . . ."

"That makes me feel better," said Krall gladly, and they got down to work.

Izolda R. began to tell Krall about her life, in other words explaining what one human being is capable of doing for another out of love.

Her life story was really an account of how she had rebelled against every decision that the Lord God made for her.

Krall did not know how to write a novel for Holly-wood, especially one in which Elizabeth Taylor was to play the central character. But she had a good friend who was a movie director, whose films had become world famous. When for political reasons she had chosen not to write for the weekly journal *Polityka* anymore, she had worked with him on his movies. His name was Krzysztof Kieślowski, and he would know how to write for Hollywood.

"Not bad," said Kieślowski, when she told him the story. "What's more," he added, "by now the American Jews have had enough of Jews as victims, Jews being humiliated and meekly dragged to their death. Your heroine fights and wins—and that's a fashionable theme, perfect for an American producer."

She asked Kieślowski to write the start of the novel for Hollywood for her. She told him some more about Izolda R.'s husband.

"His hands were straight out of an album of Italian art, as drawn by Leonardo da Vinci," wrote Kieślowski. "How on earth did Leonardo know that this very man would have hands like these? And that she—who now and then as a child, when her father was out of the house, would climb onto a chair and fetch the album down from the top shelf just to look at those hands—would meet them and touch them? Slender, distinctive hands with long fingers, the perfect place for a golden wedding ring . . ."

So the book was started, and it was evidently bound to be a love story.

When the book, titled "How Izolda Won the War," was ready, writer and heroine met up in Vienna. "It's awfully short," fretted Izolda R. She had told the author she wanted a fat book, hadn't she? The kind that would stand out on the shelf in a large American apartment.

"It was meant to be a big fat volume, but it's come out as a skinny booklet," she complained.

Poland's leading author of true-life stories explained to her that the book was exactly as it should be. When she wrote *Shielding the Flame*, a book about the Warsaw Ghetto Uprising and one of its leaders, Marek Edelman, it came out sixty pages shorter than the one about Izolda. And yet it had been translated into many languages worldwide. And the uprising was a historical event, of greater importance than Izolda's love for her husband.

"Everything I suffered was so awful," said Izolda R. "My despair, my emotions, my tears—but in your version? Just a couple of sentences. Is that really all?"

"The greater the despair, the fewer sentences are needed," explained Krall.

"But I told you such a lot . . ." said Izolda R., angry by now.

She was behaving like a client who has given a tailor some material, expecting a creation with pleats, tucks, frills, and flounces, but who's given a simple, modest dress instead.

"The richer the material, the simpler the style should be," said Krall.

Add, add, add, demanded the heroine.

Subtract, subtract, subtract, responded the author, and every time she added a sentence merely to meet the client's wishes, she soon deleted it again.

For decades Izolda R. came to Poland at least once a year. Every time she told Hanna Krall that there were too few emotions and too few words in the book.

"I felt more and more sorry for her," says Krall. "But I couldn't write the way she wanted. It was contrary to my reception of the world. It would have been insincere. The readers would immediately have sensed it, and they'd have lost confidence in me. Using a form that lies is just as bad as fabricating the content."

I am a student of Hanna Krall, and sometimes I receive short text messages from her. For instance: "Mariusz, does the world need quite so many words from you? Always ask yourself that before you start to write."

How are we to describe the Holocaust nowadays? How are we to describe Rwanda or Afghanistan? Attempts are made in various forms, but Krall has found her own prescription. "This method is in harmony with my nature," she says. "I drop the literary quality, the embellishment of words and metaphors."

She refers to a painting by Mondrian called *New York*. It consists of vertical and horizontal lines. Just as these lines are art, so art can consist of simple sentences without ornament.

In her book of essays *Der König verneigt sich und tötet* (The king bows and kills), the Nobel prize-winning author Herta Müller deconstructs Krall's method as follows:

Hanna Krall refuses to give us any commentary; her gathering and arrangement of facts gives rise to an unwavering directness that begins to reverberate in the brain. The author's documented realities apparently narrate themselves. But it is the genius of Hanna Krall to eschew all commentary, yet by way of an invisible interference to stand behind every sentence.[*]

Polish critic Michał Cichy has called Krall's work "documentary fables," in reference to the idea that humanity should record the trauma of the Holocaust in a new form of myth, in a sort of sacred book, to transmit the "truest of all truths." This myth should be documentary, referring to facts and witnesses, and avoiding fiction. Just like Hanna Krall's accounts.

A fable only has one hero, with whom we can identify, whereas we cannot identify with a million people. But we know that the hero of the fable is symbolic, representing more than just him or herself. The fable can tell us about terrible danger, but it allows us to triumph over it. It is written in a simple style—the way Krall's books are written, deceptively similar to fairy tales. In many of them, as in fairy tales, miracles occur, such as miraculously surviving the Holocaust. And these miracles really did happen.

---

[*] Quotation translated by W. Martin.

Although Krall still calls herself a reporter, she is a writer whose books have appeared in eighty translations worldwide.

Unfortunately, one of her books, "How Izolda Won the War," has never been published. For eighteen years it lay on the shelf—the heroine was dissatisfied, and the writer had lost the heart for it. It was a mixture of what Izolda wanted and what Krall wanted. Meanwhile, from one year to the next the heroine was losing her sight and hearing.

"Time I wrote my own book about you," said Krall. "Tailored just as my nature tells me."

Izolda R. eagerly agreed for *Chasing the King of Hearts* to be Krall's book, and not hers. Maybe she was hoping that this version would be a novel for Hollywood?

Chasing the King of Hearts has now been translated into all the major European languages, and when it first appeared in English, the British newspaper the *Guardian* described it as a masterpiece.

Sometimes I travel with Hanna Krall to her public events in Europe. I have sometimes heard her correct people's assumptions about her.

In France, one of the journalists said: "You write about the Holocaust . . ."

To which Krall replied: "No, I don't. All my books are about how very good human beings can be, and about how very bad they can be—something we are constantly discovering, over and over again."

In the Czech Republic, one of the journalists said: "You write about Polish-Jewish relations . . ."

To which Krall replied: "No, I don't. If I write about relations of any kind, they're between man and God."

She doesn't like it when her writing is reduced to "the Jewish theme." As if there were a separate theme for Jews and about Jews.

So she should be pleased when her works are described as documentary fables. The story of Izolda R. is definitely a fable of this kind.

In her interviews she often says that she isn't actually the author of the stories she writes. Their real author is the Great Scriptwriter. Before she got to them, he composed them and gave them meaning.

—MARIUSZ SZCZYGIEŁ, 2017
Translated by Antonia Lloyd-Jones

Apart from conversations with Hanna Krall, my sources were:

Cichy, Michał. 1999. "Baśnie dokumentalne Hanny Krall" [Hanna Krall's documentary fables]. *Gazeta Wyborcza*, January 23.

Krall, Hanna. 2015. "Powieść dla Hollywood" [A novel for Hollywood]. In *Krall*, edited by Wojciech Tochman and Mariusz Szczygieł. Warsaw: Fundacja Instytutu Reportazu.

Müller, Herta. 2003. *Der König verneigt sich und tötet* [The king bows and kills]. Munich: Carl Hanser Verlag.

Translator's Note

Hanna Krall is a master of movement, a choreographer of prose. She lays a path then cuts out words so each scene becomes a stepping-stone inviting us to constantly jump and turn, and with each new landing we gain a new perspective. Everything is flowing; time and space converge. There is Heraclitus and there is Einstein.

This book does not report: it unfolds, at a pace accelerated by the nonstop present tense and the tension of the prose. The laconic style of the original is reinforced by the language itself: Polish does not use articles, and often the subject of a sentence can be inferred from the context or implied from the grammar. The challenge is to find language taut and tensile enough to contain the silences. This is as much a matter of rhythm as of vocabulary—a problem I'm very familiar with from my work in the theater. In the translation I have made a deliberate effort to streamline the English, but only after first attempting to capture the full meaning of the Polish sentences. Consequently, the English is differently laconic than the Polish.

What lures us ahead and keeps us on course are the voices. The narrative voice, the voice of Izolda, and the voices she encounters. Most are in Polish, but not all: we also hear German, Yiddish, Russian, French, English, and Hebrew—all through her ears. Polish readers are quite accustomed to foreign encounters, so these phrases do not stand out quite as much in the original as they do in English. In some cases I have offered English equivalents, but by and large I have chosen to preserve these snippets of other languages, partly as a reminder that the war and the Holocaust were tragically multicultural.

Finally there is the question of veracity. Hanna Krall is as adept with detailed etching as she is with broad brushwork. The fact that all this actually happened makes research both helpful and necessary. Helpful because uncovering concrete facts can resolve ambiguities that might not stop the Polish reader but require some reworking in English, and necessary because these same dates and places need to match the historical record.

Passages in Hebrew were originally translated from the Polish by Michał Sobelman; I would like to thank Riva Hocherman for her help rendering these dialogues into English. And I am particularly grateful to Elżbieta Skłodowska for shedding light on what I initially found obscure.

—PHILIP BOEHM, 2017

The Feminist Press is a nonprofit educational organization founded to amplify feminist voices. FP publishes classic and new writing from around the world, creates cutting-edge programs, and elevates silenced and marginalized voices in order to support personal transformation and social justice for all people.

See our complete list of books at
feministpress.org